Goosebumps

THE VANISHED RETURN

BASED ON THE SCHOLASTIC BOOK SERIES BY R.L. STINE

KATE HOWARD

Scholastic Inc.

Copyright © 2025 Scholastic Inc.™ & © Scholastic Inc. SCHOLASTIC, GOOSEBUMPS, and associated logos are trademarks and/or registered marks of Scholastic Inc. All rights reserved.

All rights reserved. Published by Scholastic Inc., *Publishers since 1920*. SCHOLASTIC and associated logos are trademarks and/or registered trademarks of Scholastic Inc.

The publisher does not have any control over and does not assume any responsibility for author or third-party websites or their content.

No part of this publication may be reproduced, stored in a retrieval system, or transmitted in any form or by any means, electronic, mechanical, photocopying, recording, or otherwise, or used to train any artificial intelligence technologies, without written permission of the publisher. For information regarding permission, write to Scholastic Inc., Attention: Permissions Department, 557 Broadway, New York, NY 10012.

This book is a work of fiction. Names, characters, places, and incidents are either the product of the author's imagination or are used fictitiously, and any resemblance to actual persons, living or dead, business establishments, events, or locales is entirely coincidental.

ISBN 978-1-5461-5432-7

10 9 8 7 6 5 4 3 2 1   25 26 27 28 29

Printed in the U.S.A. 40
First printing 2025

Book design by Jeff Shake

PROLOGUE

FORT JEROME, GRAVESEND, BROOKLYN, 1994

*N*ight crept behind the group as they walked purposefully along the seawall in Gravesend, Brooklyn. The four teens were on a mission: to break into the old military fortress that had stood in their neighborhood since the Civil War era, crumbling more with each year that passed.

Glancing behind him to check that no one had followed them, Matty—a natural-born leader and the mastermind of their mission—led his friends down a set of spiral stairs into the lower level of the old fortress. Behind him, the other three crept along quietly, hoping not to disturb whatever horrors might be hiding inside the ancient structure. One girl in the group held a camcorder up to her face as they made their way deeper and deeper into the labyrinth, capturing their journey on tape so they could prove what they'd accomplished after they were out of Fort Jerome, safe and sound.

"C'mon," Matty said, motioning over his shoulder for the others to follow. "It's this way."

His friends followed single file under the dilapidated stone archways that were covered with dirt and moss. The girl with the camcorder lurked at the rear, capturing the others and the environment in full, vivid detail.

Matty stepped out from under the final archway and pointed across a dirt clearing. "That's the entrance," he whispered, squinting to see the outline of a tunnel that had been carved into the side of the hill directly in front of them.

"To what *exactly?*" his friend Sameer asked. He was a skater boy, all tough talk and guts when it came to tricks on his board—but this was something else altogether. Most things didn't scare him, but this did.

Matty replied, "You'll see." He flipped on his flashlight and entered the dark tunnel, with the others following close on his heels. Sameer picked up the rear, but hustled to catch up to the others when he realized they'd moved farther into the tunnel without him.

The tunnel was long and narrow, barely high enough to stand up at full height. As the group crept deeper underground, it grew darker and more ominous. Suddenly, a faint sound echoed off the walls around them as they took a few more steps into the terrifying tunnel. "Did you hear that?" their friend Nicole asked, her body stiffening as she stood still to listen for any additional sounds.

"Yeah," Sameer said, trying to play it cool. "That's the sound of us wasting our Saturday night."

"I'm serious," Nicole said, her voice now shaking just a bit. She fixed Matty with a look and asked, "You sure no one's in here?"

"Depends," Matty said, his mouth quirking up into a smirk. "Do you consider ghosts people?"

Nicole swatted at him and groaned. "Thanks. That's reassuring."

They continued on, heading for a turn up ahead. As soon as they'd come around the corner, the narrow walls of the tunnel opened into an underground bunker–type space. Equipment from decades earlier sat gathering dust on shelving along the walls. It was clear no one had been inside the bunker in many, many years.

"Okay," Matty said, his voice hushed. "This is the room where it all went down."

Nicole looked around in awe. "Where the experiments happened?"

Matty nodded. "Yep. They supposedly put people through all sorts of weird medical testing."

Nicole studied the equipment lining the walls of the long-forgotten space. "Like giving a guy two brains?" she asked, repeating a piece of the legend that had been passed on through the generations.

"Exactly," Matty said. "And they all died. It's been haunted ever since."

Sameer tried to remain calm, but standing in a space where all kinds of people had supposedly died—in the name of "science"—was seriously creepy. "Okay, Mulder," he said, nudging Matty. "I'm not buying it. Anyway, this dare doesn't seem like a great idea anymore."

"Are you scared?" Matty taunted, knowing full well his friend's tough-guy persona was an act.

"I don't like sleeping on hard surfaces," Sameer said with a shrug. "You know that about me. What if we just left and said we slept over. Who would know?"

"Everybody," Matty said. He pointed at their friend with the camcorder, the device's little red light flashing as a reminder that it was recording everything. "That's why we brought her."

A laugh came from the girl behind the camera. "Haha."

Matty looked directly into the camera and asked, "You are recording all this, right?"

She gave him a thumbs-up and took another sweep of the room from behind the camera lens. As the light shining from the camera illuminated a wall of equipment, the shelves suddenly tipped over and crashed to the ground.

All four of the teens jumped back, terrified and screaming after the sudden sound.

Matty stepped forward, shining his light into the area to figure out what might have toppled the shelf. "Stink!" he growled, spotting his little brother looking guilty and up to no good as he tried to hide in the shadows. Fourteen-year-old Stink was not supposed to be here, and he knew it.

Matty yanked his brother to his feet and dragged him out of the bunker, through the tunnel, and back to the secret entrance. Once they were outside, Matty wheeled on the younger boy and snapped, "I cannot believe you followed us. Mom is going to blame this on me!"

Stink grinned, turning on his full charm. "Mom won't know."

"She will if you don't go home." Matty sighed. "Now, Stink."

"I hate that nickname," Stink retorted, trying to buy himself a little more time.

"Just go," Matty said, turning back toward the mouth of the tunnel.

"It's kind of scary out here," Stink said, surveying the crumbling fortress around them.

"It's scarier in there," Matty said, then he stepped inside the tunnel to rejoin his friends on their mission, leaving his brother at the entrance. Once he was back in the bunker, he found the other three teenagers huddled around the damaged wall of equipment, studying something. "Sorry about that, guys—" he began, but Sameer cut him off.

"Hey," Sameer said. "Check this out." He gestured to the fallen wall of equipment. Old transformers were embedded inside the wall, and they were glowing with electricity. "This stuff still has power going to it," he said, pointing. "I wonder what it does?"

Suddenly, the transformers popped and shorted out. Moments later, a hidden circular hatch descended from the floor, opening up into a mysterious underground area. A rush of air escaped from the hatch, which reminded Matty of the sound tombs made when they were being opened (at least in the movies he'd watched).

Matty walked across the room and peered into the hole. "There's something down there," he said, squinting for a better look.

"I mean," Sameer said, shrugging, "there's something down everywhere—"

"Well, what is it?" Matty asked.

"I don't know," Nicole told the others. "But I found something in this flask." She held up an old metal flask filled with some kind of liquid. How old it was, no one could possibly know.

"I'm going to check it out," Matty declared, stepping over the hole in the floor. "Aim all your flashlights straight down." As the others shined their flashlights at Matty, he lowered himself through the open hatch into the space below. Almost instantly, the darkness swallowed him up and he disappeared from view.

"Do you think it's rude if we leave?" Sameer asked the two girls.

The answer came from behind the camera: "Shhhhh."

Seconds passed in silence while they all waited for a sound, some sign, any signal from their friend that he was okay. Suddenly, there were scrambling sounds and Matty reappeared through the hole. He quickly pulled himself up and out, his expression terrified.

"What did you see?" Sameer asked.

"I don't know . . ." Matty said softly, shaking his head.

"What do you mean?" Nicole demanded. "What's down there?"

Matty stared back, his face blank. "I don't know!" He was more serious than any of his friends had seen him before. Suddenly, his body went rigid and he said, "Dare's over. We're leaving." He turned to lead the group back out through the tunnel. But before he could take two steps, the light from the camcorder illuminated a cluster of strange-looking black spores that were stuck to Matty's hoodie.

"What's that?" Nicole said, reeling back a bit.

Matty looked around in confusion.

"On your sweatshirt," Sameer explained, pointing.

Matty looked down and saw the spores attached to his clothing. But when he tried to brush them off, they stuck to his hands instead. A few floated into the air, hovering in the murky space around him. A low hum began to emanate from somewhere within the room, and all four teens froze.

"Do you guys hear that?" Nicole asked nervously.

The camcorder nodded up and down in agreement.

"It's getting louder," Sameer noted.

Turning in place, trying to find the source of the sound, Nicole suddenly staggered backward. "Matty," she whispered. "Your face."

The others spun around to see what she was talking about. Tears were pouring from Matty's eyes, but they weren't regular tears—these tears were pure black. As the light from the camcorder caught the others' faces, each of them realized it wasn't just Matty weeping black tears. They all were.

A scream tore through the fort as the black goo began to pour from the eyes, ears, noses, and mouths of all four teens. There was a faint hiss as the goo began to eat through their flesh, and soon Matty's skeletal form was exposed in the center of the dark bunker, his friends left to the same fate.

The screaming in Fort Jerome cut off abruptly. The room was empty. The camcorder was lying on the ground, its light still shining. The only other thing left of the teens was their empty clothes, crumpled in heaps on the floor, as if the inhabitants had just up and vanished. The four friends were gone.

CHAPTER ONE

GRAVESEND, BROOKLYN, 2024

Cece and Devin Brewer lugged their suitcases up the steep stair-case leading from the subway station. The train had just deposited them in their father's neighborhood in Brooklyn, where they would be spending the summer.

Divorce was rough for a lot of reasons, but as far as Cece was concerned, this banishment to the outermost edge of Brooklyn was possibly the worst part of her parents' divorce. "This is, like, really far away from New York," she muttered to her brother, lips pursing to take a quick sip of her kombucha. She gingerly stepped over a pile of dog poop on the sidewalk and averted her gaze so she didn't have to look at the very old woman slurping food out of a packet of tinfoil. She brushed her highlighted hair over one shoulder and her brown eyes narrowed into a squint. Cece was the definition of a polished, always-put-together city girl, and this was very much *not* the city.

Devin glanced over at his sister, his blueish eyes sparkling. Though they were twins, they didn't look much alike aside from their slender builds and matching AirPods (to listen to *very* different styles of music)—and they certainly didn't *act* anything alike. The two twins couldn't be more different. Where Cece saw *gross*, Devin saw beauty—the graffiti, the old woman enjoying her meal right in the heart of the neighborhood. He was into *all* of it. "Brooklyn is still New York, Cece," Devin reminded her.

"Brooklyn is still New York," Cece mocked in a strange voice, rolling her eyes as she tried to focus on her calming podcast instead of the awful surroundings.

"Doing a dumb voice doesn't make it any less true—" Devin said, shrugging.

Cece cut him off. "You're right. When Emma Lazarus said, 'Give me your tired, your poor,' she was imagining this hot, gross subway station." She took another swig of kombucha, trying to erase the smell of urine that was coming from somewhere nearby.

"You are such a snob," Devin noted.

"No, I'm *honest*, Devin," Cece sighed. "And Gravesend, Brooklyn, isn't even cool Brooklyn. Does it seem hotter here?" She waved a hand in front of her face, noting the rivulet of sweat running down her back, even though she was perfectly dressed for a hot New York summer day. "It seems hotter here."

"It seems the same amount of hot," Devin said, giving his suitcase a tug.

Cece glanced down at her Apple Watch for verification. "Yep, it's hotter here. And it smells worse."

Devin gestured with his chin. "And there's a dead rat."

"Where?" Cece shrieked.

"Got you," Devin chuckled. "But I'm sure there is one."

"Why couldn't we have stayed in our apartment?" Cece

whined. "It's just sitting there empty. Near friends. And parties. And all the things that, like, *happen*."

Suddenly, a loud car horn cut through the din of the neighborhood. Cece and Devin glanced up to catch their dad, Anthony Brewer, waving to them from inside the driver's seat of his electric Volvo. "Hey, guys!" their dad called, rolling down his window.

"Hi," Cece said with a limp wave.

"Hey, Dad," Devin called back.

Anthony hopped out of the car to give them each a quick hug. Cece cringed when she saw what was on the front of his shirt: a cute plant and the words *Say aloe to my little friend.*

"Best. Summer. Ever! Already twinning," Anthony said, his joy at seeing his kids immediately obvious.

"That's not how you use that," Cece noted, watching as her dad tossed her luggage into the trunk of his car. She slid into the air-conditioned front seat as her brother helped to load his own suitcase into the back.

"We could have just walked," Devin told his dad, not wanting to be a bother. "The house is, like, three blocks from here."

"I wasn't gonna make you walk with your luggage," Anthony told him, patting his son on the shoulder. It had been hard since the divorce, not seeing the twins every day the way he wished he could. But being out here now—living in and caring for his mom's old house, now his, in Gravesend—gave him plenty of time and space to do his work as a botanist. Plants were sort of like Anthony's other babies; he loved his job and the research it entailed.

Devin began to walk around the back of the car to climb into the backseat, but his dad put his hand out to stop him. "Get in on the sidewalk side. It's safer."

A few minutes later, they pulled up in front of the Brewers' small, simple house on a quiet street not far from the subway station—only to find an old 1994 Oldsmobile blocking the entrance to the driveway. Anthony honked, but nothing happened. Clearly, the car wasn't about to drive away on its own.

Cece and Devin hopped out of the car, while Anthony honked again. A few minutes later, a muscular tough guy who lived across the street from Anthony came strolling out of his house. "What?" he snapped.

"Trey, you're blocking my driveway. Again," Anthony sighed. "I thought I made it clear that you can't do that." Anthony popped the trunk and the kids grabbed their bags to head up to the porch to watch their dad's disagreement play out.

"Your mom always let me park there," Trey said, his voice dripping with disrespect. He was the kind of guy who was used to getting what he wanted, and he wasn't going to take some weeny, plant-obsessed, middle-aged white guy's whining about where he could and couldn't park his beauty of a car.

Anthony sighed again. "She didn't have a car," he reminded Trey. "So you weren't blocking anything. Also, she had dementia. I really don't want to talk to your father about this."

Trey wasn't afraid of much, but this was the one threat that would work on him. He *also* didn't want Anthony talking to his dad about their beef. "Fine," he grumbled. "Give me a minute." He headed back inside his house to grab his keys.

Meanwhile, Anthony explained, "That's Joe Junior's son, Joe the third."

"So . . ." Cece said, doing the math. "He's Joe Junior Junior? We really are a long way from home." Anthony led them up the stairs and unlocked the front door for his kids just as Trey returned with car keys.

"That guy sucks," Devin said, taking his dad's side.

"Don't say stuff like that," Anthony scolded. But after another second, he muttered, "But you're not wrong."

Inside the house, Cece and Devin took everything in. Anthony had clearly not moved in fully, as there were unpacked boxes everywhere. He'd been working hard to clean out and organize his mom's stuff, but all those boxes were intermingled with his own and the place was a bit cluttered. "Since I moved Grandma into the home, I've been going through all her things," Anthony explained, gesturing to years' worth of boxes and bins. "Sorting, organizing—"

Cece cut him off. "Mostly throwing away?"

Anthony laughed. "Yeah, that, too." He took a deep breath and studied his kids. He was glad he'd focused on getting their rooms ready for the summer, since he wanted this to be a great time for all of them together. "I've been really looking forward to your stepdad's back surgery," he said, then cringed when he realized how that sounded. "I mean, since it meant you guys were coming here. I set up both bedrooms with futons. They are mostly the same. One of them is just less teal."

Devin raised his eyebrows and looked to his sister. "Flip for it?"

Anthony added, "I want you guys to have a fun, but also safe, summer out here. And honestly, I only have one rule other than the list of rules I put in your bedrooms, and that is: Stay out of the basement."

Cece smirked. "Now I *have* to see the basement."

Begrudgingly, Anthony led his kids downstairs to his lab. This was his pride and joy, the one place he loved more than anywhere else on Earth. It was stuffed, floor to ceiling, with equipment and instruments and plants—*everywhere*. The only empty space on the walls had been covered with a *Botanic Action* poster of Anthony's botany hero and mentor, David Bellamy, hugging a cactus.

"Staying out of here won't be a problem," Cece mused.

"Yeah," Devin agreed. "It's kind of giving villain-origin-story vibes."

"Or dispensary vibes," Cece said.

Anthony laughed. "I can't talk about it yet," he said, his excitement bubbling up. "But I may have stumbled upon a new totipotent embryophyte that could rock the botany world."

Cece furrowed her eyebrows. "The botany world can be 'rocked'?"

"In certain specific instances," Anthony said, all seriousness, "yes, it can be. I don't know if 'rocked' is the right nomenclature. Maybe . . . disrupt?"

"Wow, Dad," Devin said, equally serious. "That's great." He leaned in to touch one of the ferns that had vines dripping down from its hydroponic planter bin.

Anthony slapped his hand away. "No touching!" Both kids' mouths opened in surprise. It was a bit of an overreaction for a *plant*. Even Anthony seemed to realize it was harsh, and he tried to diffuse the awkward moment with a joke. "Why should you never look under ferns?" He waited for them to guess, but neither Cece nor Devin had any idea where their dad was going with this. "You'll get sore eye. Sori is what they call fern spores. And you look for them underneath—" He broke off, then pulled his kids in for an awkward hug. "Look at us, back together again. Like Brunfels, Fuchs, and Bock. The three fathers of botany!"

Cece shook her head and pulled away. "I'm starving."

"Me too," Devin agreed.

Anthony nodded. "Let's go out for dinner. To celebrate. I know a great place. Well, it's a convenient place."

As they headed upstairs from the basement botany lab, Cece and Devin both considered how this summer was going to play out. Their dad was really something, and this basement—well, it was even *more*. Luckily, neither of them was remotely tempted to revisit his precious lab again. And as long as they could respect that rule, surely nothing could possibly go wrong this summer.

CHAPTER TWO

T he restaurant was right around the corner, and it was certainly *convenient*, but not *great*. The neighborhood family restaurant made up for its lack of charm with overwhelming redness—from the chairs to the walls.

While they ate, Anthony pressed his kids for information, hoping to get caught up on their lives and all he'd missed the past few months. "So, Cece," he began, "you're going to debate camp starting Monday? Back in the city?"

"Yep," Cece said, taking a bite of her meal.

"It's just a day camp, right?" Anthony confirmed. He didn't love that she was going to have to commute back to Manhattan every day for this debate camp. He wished both kids could just hang out around Gravesend, getting a different summer experience than they got when they spent the summer in the hustle of the city.

"Yep," Cece said again.

"You looking forward to it?" he asked.

"Yep."

"Any other details you want to provide?"

"Nope," Cece said, then took another bite of her mediocre meal.

"That should be fun," Anthony said, all false cheer.

Cece looked up and glared at him. "Fun?" she snapped. "No, debate camp is not *fun*. It's like the smartest people all getting together and telling you why you're wrong. It's super intense, but it's my thing. And you have to have a *thing* to get into college."

"Isn't the whole point of college to figure out your thing, while racking up extreme amounts of debt?" Devin asked, knowing this would push his twin sister's buttons.

"It used to be," Cece said bitterly. "Now you have to figure out your thing to even get into college. Then once there, you pivot to a new thing. I don't even know why I have to explain this." She pushed her chair back and stood, then headed to the restroom.

"I didn't realize it was this bad—" Anthony began.

Devin rolled his eyes. "She's just being extra, Dad."

"Okay," Anthony said, perking up. "And you, how're you doing?"

"Everything's coo'." Devin said with an easy smile.

"I mean," Anthony said tentatively, "given the whole thing that happened—"

Devin stiffened. "I said I'm coo'."

Anthony narrowed his eyes. "You got suspended for fighting, Devin. That isn't 'coo'."

"That guy started it," Devin snapped.

"That doesn't mean you have to finish it. You need to learn to back down sometimes." Anthony knew this was a sore spot for his son, but it was something they had to talk about. He was his father, after all. But based on the reaction he'd gotten from both of his kids when he'd tried to press into their lives, he had a feeling this summer was going to get off to a slightly rockier start than he'd anticipated.

As the three of them left the restaurant a short while later, they nearly bumped into CJ, the restaurant's delivery kid. He'd pulled his electric scooter up alongside the restaurant's exterior and was heading inside for his next order. "Anthony!" CJ said, holding his hand up for a high five. "The Plant Man."

"Hey, CJ," Anthony said. "These are my kids, Cece and Michael Devin."

"MD!" CJ said to Devin, grinning his megawatt smile. It was obvious he was one of those instantly likable people—friendly, charming, and easygoing.

"Just Devin," Devin said, glaring at his dad.

CJ took off his helmet, revealing dark, close-cropped hair underneath. His brown skin was covered in a sheen of sweat from riding around in the summer heat, which made his whole face glow. "Oh, right," he said, pointing at them. "The twins. Fraternal." He smiled at Cece in a flirtatious way.

"What was that?" Cece said, taking none of what he was dishing out.

"CJ's working here for his parents this summer," Anthony explained. "Devin, maybe you could get a job, too. Since you don't really have anything going on."

Just then, CJ's mom popped her head out the front door, holding a bag of takeout. "Where have you been?" she snapped at her son. "People have been calling and complaining about late food all night!"

"Mom," CJ groaned. "It's not my fault." As his mom retreated back inside the restaurant, CJ whispered loudly, "You do *not* want to work here. Management sucks."

"I heard that!" his mom yelled from inside the restaurant.

"Good!" CJ yelled back. He backed his scooter up, preparing to head out for his next delivery. But first, he turned to the twins and said, "Hey, Trey's throwing a party tomorrow night. Everyone will be there. You guys should come by. I'm kind of like the don of Gravesend. I can show you what is what and who is who. See you there!" As he hopped on his scooter, he pulled an egg roll out of the bag and took a bite.

"Did he just eat out of that delivery bag?" Cece asked as CJ drove away.

Anthony led his kids around the corner toward their house and ushered them through the front door as an unmarked police car pulled into the driveway.

"What's going on?" Cece asked, gesturing to the cop car.

"I don't know," Anthony told them. "Just wait for me inside."

As they headed inside the house, Cece muttered to her brother, "Maybe the basement *is* a dispensary."

"Dispensaries are legal now," Devin told her.

"I know that," Cece said, rolling her eyes.

"Sorry." Devin shrugged. "I don't know what nerds know and don't know."

As soon as the kids were inside, Anthony stepped off the porch and greeted the female officer who'd just gotten out of the car. It was his friend Jen, with whom he had a *long* history.

She tipped her chin up at him in a greeting and said, "Joe Junior stopped by the station today. He tried to file a harassment complaint on behalf of his son."

Anthony scoffed. "Harassment complaint? Trey's been blocking *my* driveway."

Jen shrugged. "He says he had an arrangement with your mom. I'm sorry, by the way."

Anthony shook his head. "She's not dead."

"I know," Jen said, quickly backtracking. "I didn't . . . look, I'm just here as a courtesy, okay? I'll go talk to Joe Junior and calm things down."

He nodded. "Thanks. I better get inside. My kids are staying with me."

Jen glanced up at the window, catching both the twins watching their exchange through the window. "I heard. That's great. I'm happy for you, Stink."

Anthony froze, memories flooding him with ice when he heard his old childhood name. "I hate that nickname, Jen."

"Sorry," Jen said. "Old habit. Have a good night."

CHAPTER THREE

"I am not the one who signed her up for debate camp in the city," Anthony snarled into the phone, pacing to try to walk off the frustration from talking to his ex-wife. "Yes, I know kids take the train all the time by themselves, but it's a long way. I just think that's the kind of thing you discuss with a co-parent. Since that's what we are. *Co-*, Latin for 'join, jointly, together.'" He paused, listening to his kids' mom lecturing him on the other end of the phone. "No, you're right. I'm *not* paying for it. I put my whole career on pause because my mother has dementia. It wasn't like a fun choice! Do *you* have a job? Or are you still living off your parents' money?"

He hung up, then spun around to find that Devin had been listening to the whole conversation. "Don't worry," Anthony told him with a sigh. "We can't get divorced twice."

"That's a relief," Devin said.

"Hey, look," Anthony went on. "Sometimes I forget that your mom wants the same things I want for you; we just have a different way of getting there."

Cece stepped into the kitchen before he could say more. "What's that smell?" she asked, sniffing.

"I made you guys breakfast—waffles. They're in the toaster," Anthony said, gesturing to the appliance just as four burned, charred waffles popped up.

Devin and Cece looked to each other and, at the same time, said, "Bagels." At least this was one thing they were totally on the same page about.

Anthony pulled a twenty out of his wallet and held it out to them. "And here you go."

The twins headed down Gravesend's main street, on the hunt for a breakfast that wasn't ruined. While they walked, Devin said, "I think we should go to that stoop party later."

Cece smirked at him. "Because you think Frankie will be there?" She waggled her eyebrows.

"CJ said *everyone* will be there," Devin retorted. "And I am not going to apologize for being a human man with passion."

"Gross."

Devin shrugged. "These are facts. I am attracted to Frankie, and I believe she will still be attracted to me—"

Cece cut him off. "The last time we were here, we were fourteen." She glanced at her brother and could tell he was not going to back down from the idea of going to Trey's party. "Fine. I'll go. There's nothing else to do around here. Just don't overuse the word *bussin'*. Nobody says that anymore."

"It's retro," Devin noted.

"Not in a good way," Cece told him.

"Whatever. It could be fun. You might meet someone, too. Your Pedro Pascal could be just around the corner."

Cece snorted. "I've moved on to Elordi."

"Who's going to break it to Pedro?" He stopped in front of a pharmacy and said, "Oh, let's go in here." He needed some product to make himself look good for Frankie that night. It had been years since he'd last seen her, and he was hoping to make a good impression. Maybe they could finally have a chance at something. He held up two hair products for his sister to evaluate. "Okay, which styling product says, 'I care, but not too much'? Also, do I need conditioner? And what kind of soap do we buy? I have never really noticed. Is it just called 'soap'?"

"It's just a house party, Devin," Cece reminded him. "Not the Met Gala."

Cece wandered toward the makeup aisle while her brother continued to fret over products. Suddenly, a disruption at the end of the aisle caught her attention. "No, no, no!" The store manager was shouting at someone. "You get out of here!" The manager was yelling at a skinny girl around Cece's age who was covered in tattoos and whose face was deliberately frozen in an uninterested expression. Despite the sour expression, it was immediately clear that she was gorgeous—dark curls, light brown skin, and a lush pink pout. "Out!" the store's manager yelled again, gesturing at the girl. "Now!"

"C'mon, man," the girl said, rolling her eyes. "I just need Advil."

"I don't care! Get out of here!"

The girl glared at the store manager. "That's discrimination," she said, pulling out her phone. She began to record, and said, "I'm going live! Right now, this person is discriminating against me."

"No, I'm going live," the store manager said, pulling out his own phone.

While the two continued to bicker, Cece took the opportunity to slip a lip gloss into her purse. The girl at the end of the aisle raised her eyebrows, showing she'd seen *exactly* what Cece had done—but she didn't rat her out. Instead, she turned to the store manager and said, "You know what? I get it. You don't want a criminal element in here. I'll respect your wishes." She shrugged, then left the store.

As Cece watched the girl leave, her brother came up behind her with a bottle of something in his hand. "Do you think a twenty-year-old bottle of Hungarian baby shampoo is okay?"

That night, the twins hit up the party as planned. The place was packed; people were hanging out on the stoop, in the driveway, and around Trey himself, who was perched on the hood of his precious Oldsmobile.

As Cece and Devin walked across the street to join in, Devin muttered, "This is . . . cool?"

Cece sighed. "I wouldn't go that far." Before they'd made it all the way across the yard, CJ appeared and handed them both red Solo cups.

"Devvey, Cecinator—"

"Not our nicknames," Devin said quickly.

Cece added, "No one has ever called me that."

CJ grinned. "Welcome to a Gravesend summer tradition since 1763, when Alexander Hamilton threw the first Gravesend house party. The rest is history."

"That makes no sense on literally every level," Devin told him.

CJ continued to play gracious host, even though it wasn't his party. "Would either of you care for a paper cup of slightly stale Takis Blue Heat?"

"Sure," Devin said, shrugging.

"No thanks," Cece sniffed.

"Or perhaps a sushi platter?" CJ continued.

"Really?" Cece said, perking up. "Yeah—"

"I'm joking," CJ said, nudging her shoulder. "There isn't a sushi platter for, like, ten square miles." He high-fived Devin, and they shared a laugh.

"How are you ganging up on me already?" Cece asked, leveling them both with a stare. "You don't even know each other."

"Cece, baby," CJ said smoothly. "I'm not about hate. I'm about love. It all comes from love." He draped his arm over her shoulder.

"Arm off," she said, shrugging away from him.

Just then, someone called out to them from across the party. "Devin?" Devin turned and saw the one person he'd been *hoping* would be at this party—Frankie. She was beautiful, with long dark hair that perfectly framed her wide-set brown eyes. "Devin! Cece!" She gave each of the twins a big hug, but lingered on Devin's.

CJ whispered to Cece, "Crushing hard?"

Cece nodded. "Bet."

"I didn't know you were here," Frankie said.

"We are!" Devin said loudly. "I am. I am here. We are both here." His face went flush as he realized he was rambling. Not the start he'd been hoping for.

"These are undeniable facts," Cece added. "Our existence remains indelibly in this place."

"Well, I'm glad you're in this place," Frankie said with an easy smile.

"It's bussin' out here in Gravesend," Devin said, nodding. "So bussin'.'"

His sister stifled a laugh.

"Yeah," Frankie said, nodding slowly. "I guess it is."

"I'm gonna get some—" Cece said, backing away. "Go somewhere . . . else." She walked off, grabbing CJ's arm.

"I liked that," Devin heard CJ say as his sister pulled him away. "It was like a real reality show."

Once they were gone, Frankie focused on Devin. "So," she began, "it's been a while."

"Yeah, totally," Devin agreed. "I mean, I follow you on TikTok. You have gotten *really* good at knitting."

"You watch those videos?" Frankie said, cringing.

"No," Devin sputtered. "I mean, not in, like, a weird way."

"I always forget people can see them," Frankie muttered.

Devin gave her a curious look. "That is what they're for. *Social* media. Not personal private media." He broke off, worried she was going to take that as a diss. "Bussin' . . ." He glanced at her sweater. "Did you make that?"

Frankie beamed. "I did! The problem with knitting is that in the summer, all you have is stuff that's hot."

"Well," Devin said. "It looks good."

"Shut up," Frankie said, blushing. She giggled, but then went silent when Trey came up behind her, spun her around, and planted a big kiss on her lips.

Trey glared at Devin, clearly wondering what he was doing with *his* girl. "You're Planthony's kid, right?"

"Funny," Devin said, pointing at him. "You took my dad's occupation and combined it with his name."

Trey squinted at him. It was clear he felt about Devin the same way he did about Anthony—which was, not great. Frankie cut through the awkward moment by saying, "This is my boyfriend, Trey. He's in college."

Devin nodded. "I wouldn't have guessed that." He paused, letting this sink in. "Because you look so young."

Frankie quickly continued, "And this is Devin, my buddy from way back."

"Oh, I didn't know you knew each other," Trey spat. "Does he knit, too?" He tugged Frankie's arm to pull her away, and Devin watched as Frankie left with the other guy. As he led her away, Trey cooed to Frankie, "Are you hungry, babe? Let me get you something to eat."

Across the party, Cece was surveying the scene while munching on Takis. She scanned the yard to see if her Elordi was anywhere nearby, but she didn't see any prospects. She pulled out her stolen tube of lip gloss and dabbed some on.

"I like your lip gloss," someone said, and Cece looked up to find the girl from the pharmacy looking at her, one eyebrow raised. "I'm Alex, by the way."

"Thanks," Cece replied nervously. Alex took the tube of lip

gloss out of Cece's hand and spread some on her own lips. Cece squared her shoulders and told her, "My mom says you're not supposed to share makeup. You know, germs."

Alex smirked. "Well, my mom says you're not supposed to steal. You know, laws." She handed the tube back, then strolled off, heading toward Trey's car.

Cece tossed the lip gloss in the trash, then noticed her brother heading her way. "I want to get out of here," she told him.

"Yeah," Devin agreed. "Me too." They began to head across the street toward their dad's house, but they were stopped by CJ's arms wrapping around their shoulders. "Guys, there you are. Come hang out." He spun them around and walked them back toward the party. He guided them to a group of his friends who were standing around Trey's car—including Alex, Trey, and Frankie. "You guys know that Devin and Cece's uncle was one of the kids who went missing in 1994?" CJ said by way of introduction.

It was clear this news was impressive, and everyone's attention quickly shifted to Devin and Cece.

Alex sidled over to stand beside Cece and whispered, "You're full of surprises."

"Oh my god, that story gave me nightmares when I was a kid," Frankie said, shivering. "That place is seriously haunted."

"So what was the real deal?" Alex asked.

"They just slept over on a dare," Cece said with a shrug. Truth be told, she didn't know much about what happened that night all those years ago—just that her uncle had gone missing, along with three of his friends.

"And were killed by ghosts?" Alex said.

"Nobody knows what happened," Cece told the group.

Devin nodded. "I mean, they were probably *not* killed by ghosts."

"You're not scared of that place?" Frankie asked.

Devin noticed Trey side-eyeing him. Devin shook his head. "No."

Trey smirked. "Prove it."

As soon as Trey threw down the dare, Devin realized he'd walked right into another trap—just like his dad warned him might happen. And he wasn't the kind of guy who could walk away from a challenge.

CHAPTER FOUR

Trey's Oldsmobile pulled up to Fort Jerome, the site of the mysterious 1994 disappearances, not long afterward. CJ and Devin rolled up behind them, sharing CJ's scooter. There was a tall fence surrounding the old fortress, and KEEP OUT signs were pasted everywhere along the perimeter.

"They put all these lights in after what happened," CJ told the others, pointing at the harsh security floodlights that illuminated the entire area. "They're supposed to help keep people out."

Trey popped open his trunk and reached inside. He pulled out a set of bolt cutters and walked over to the fence.

"You just *have* bolt cutters," Devin muttered. "Like, in your trunk."

"Yeah?" Trey replied casually.

"All right. Cool." Devin nodded. Trey was clearly not someone to mess with.

"Go, Gravesend," Cece said, shaking her head.

Once Trey had cut through the lock and pushed the fence open, the rest of the group filed in behind him, slipping into the fenced-off fort area. They congregated on a balcony that overlooked the path leading into the tunnels below. "The stairs are through there," Trey said, pointing to a long row of archways along the seawall. "Once you get down, you'll see the tunnel entrance. It leads to the room where your uncle and his friends died."

"How do you know all that?" Cece asked.

"There's this old *20/20* episode on YouTube that describes the whole thing," Trey explained. "They interviewed my dad." He passed his flashlight to Devin, then offered him an out. "Not too late to back down."

But Devin grabbed the flashlight and shook his head.

"This is some serious toxic masculinity stuff," Cece noted.

Alex grinned. "That's what I like about it. Let them weed each other out. The matriarchy will rise."

CJ grabbed Devin's arm. "You don't have to do this. This is a thing I need to say to you. But I'm really excited you're doing it. Because it's going to be cool." He nodded reassuringly. "Good luck." He gave Devin a bro hug.

Cece pulled her brother aside and whispered, "Devin, you don't have to do this to impress Frankie."

Devin shook his head. "I don't know if that's true, Cece. She looks pretty impressed right now."

Cece glanced over just in time to see Frankie gazing at Devin in a way that said her brother was probably right. "Okay, maybe—but you still shouldn't do this."

"I'm not letting Joe Junior Junior over there get the better of me."

"Devin, who cares?" Cece grumbled. "Just let this go."

"It's a tunnel and a room," Devin said casually. "I'll go in, take a few pictures, and come right out. It's not a big deal."

But it was a big deal. As Devin made his way along the pathway, down the spiral stairs, and into the tunnel—where his uncle died, disappeared, whatever happened to him—he realized the significance of this dare. It was terrifying, yes. Dark, creepy, ominous, all those things. But also, it was worth it. He would be a legend.

He made his way into the mouth of the tunnel, which was illuminated by ceiling lights. He glanced back and could see the others watching him. He took another step forward.

From their perch up on the balcony, the group watched Devin disappear. "I can't believe he's actually going in there," Frankie mused. "That's, like, really brave." She turned to Cece and asked, "So are you guys going to be here, like, all summer?"

"Yep, all summer." Cece grinned, first at Frankie and then at Trey—who was clearly not happy to hear this news. "Just like that summer when you and Devin became besties. I remember you kept asking him to marry you."

Frankie giggled. "He was such a cutie back then. He kept saying, 'Maybe.'"

CJ suddenly blurted out, "Man, I got to hand it to your bro. I wouldn't go in there alone. But I'm, like, a real people person."

Trey had had enough of everyone talking about how great Devin was. He suddenly moved toward an electric panel at the base of the utility pole that carried power to the entirety of Fort Jerome. He lifted his bolt cutters up and popped open the lock. "It's easy when the lights are on," he said with a menacing grin.

Devin had reached the bunker at the end of the tunnel, and he was getting more creeped out by the second. It appeared as if nothing had changed in the thirty years since his uncle had been in this very same space for his last moments on Earth. He stepped into the small space and took in the dirt and dust and old electronic devices spilling out over the floor.

Just as he was about to lift his phone to grab a few pictures proving he'd been there, the lights in the tunnel behind him flickered, and then everything went dark. "What the hell?" Devin said, scrambling to pull out Trey's flashlight. As soon as he had it on, he spun around to shine the light back into the tunnel he'd just come through. Then from behind him, Devin could hear a rush of air, like the sound of a vault being opened. He spun around and shined his light in every corner, trying to figure out where the noise had come from. That's when he spotted a circular hatch that had opened up in the floor. There was an eerie glow shining up from beneath it, and something that looked like little black spores was bubbling up from below.

Devin began to back away from the hole. But just as he spun toward the tunnel and prepared to run, his flashlight illuminated a person standing right in front of him. It was a kid, somewhere around his age, maybe, but this kid's eyes and mouth were leaking black liquid. With a stifled scream, Devin scrambled backward, then lost his footing and fell—right into the spores that had bubbled up from below. His flashlight dropped, and when it hit the ground, it flicked out, plunging Devin into complete and utter darkness.

"Turn the lights back on!" Cece snapped, getting right up in Trey's face.

Trey threw the switch on the power panel a few times, but it didn't seem to be working. He laughed. "I think I blew the transformer."

"Now I remember how much of a dick you always were," Alex noted.

"Comments are closed, juvie," Trey cracked back. Then he turned and noticed Frankie judging him. "What?" he demanded.

"You know what," Frankie said softly.

"Devin!" Cece yelled down toward the entrance to the tunnel. "You okay?" When there was no response, she told the others, "Something's wrong."

"He's got a flashlight. He'll find his way out. It's just a tunnel," Trey said, laughing.

"Yeah, even *you* could find your way out," Alex said.

Devin fumbled around in the dark, trying to find his way back to the tunnel's mouth so he could get out of there. But all around him was thick, choking blackness—and no matter which way he turned, he couldn't seem to find the way out. His heart raced thinking of the kid who had been standing there just seconds before his light had gone out. Who was it? What did they want? And was he doomed to the same fate as his uncle had been all those years ago?

Suddenly, he began to hear a low hum. In the long, terrifying moments that followed, Devin's steps grew heavier and heavier. It was getting harder and harder to move. As he staggered around in the confined space, Devin's eyes began to rain black tears. He collapsed, just a single step from the tunnel entrance, and began to shake.

"Devin!" Cece's voice pulled her brother out of whatever trance he'd fallen under. She grabbed his arm and tugged, pulling him to his feet. She dragged him through the tunnel and out into the night. As soon as she got him back to the balcony with the others, Trey asked, "He's okay, right?" The last thing he needed was more trouble—from Plant Dad or, worse, his own dad.

"I don't know," Cece said, nearly in tears.

Devin shook his head, trying to clear away the fog that had settled over him while he was inside the bunker. "I'm okay. I just fell down." He looked up and tried to muster a reassuring smile for the others.

"Oh my god, your eyes!" Frankie gasped. There were black stains all around his eyes from the tears that had been seeping from him down in the bunker.

Devin swiped at his face with his sleeve and inspected them. "It's just oil or something. But—" He grew deathly serious. "There's someone down there."

"We better go," Alex said, instantly on high alert. The group fled the scene, hustling to get out of there. But no matter how fast they moved, the nightmare that began for each of them that night was sure to follow.

CHAPTER FIVE

"How are you feeling?" Cece asked her twin brother the next morning before she left to catch her subway into the city. She was dressed for success, a picture-perfect representation of a state champion debater. "Still don't remember anything?"

"I remember going into the tunnel, and then that's it, it all goes black."

"It was really scary, Dev. Like, really, really scary."

"I'm sorry."

Cece heaved a sigh. "I am just so sick of you always doing stuff like this. What is it you're trying to prove?"

"I said I'm sorry. We're not all perfect straight-A debate students bound for Yale with our whole lives figured out."

Anthony bounded in just as Devin finished his rant, grabbing his messenger bag off the table. "The home called," he told his kids. "Your grandma had a really tough night. She's very agitated. I gotta get over there. You guys should come. It'll be good for her to see you."

"Sorry," Cece said with a shrug. "No can do. First day of debate camp."

Devin threw his sister a bitter look. "I'll go."

When they arrived later that morning, the retirement home proved to be even worse than Devin had imagined. He and his dad were guided into his grandmother's small room, where they found his grandma pacing and clearly very upset. She was clutching a resealable plastic bag in her hands, with an old hoodie stuffed inside. "Matty! Matty!" Grandma Naomi wailed.

"Ma," Anthony said, racing to her. "Ma, you gotta calm down."

"We have to find Matty, Anthony!" Grandma sobbed.

"Ma, you know Matty is gone. Remember the fort on the water? They drowned. It's the only explanation—"

"No!" Grandma said, growling at him. "Matty was the best swimmer. The *best* swimmer." She held up the plastic bag and shook it in the air again. "You have to find him!"

"I wish you didn't bring this stuff when you moved in here," Anthony said, gingerly prying the bag out of his mom's hands. "It just upsets you. Now breathe in, breathe out. It's gonna be okay, Ma, you hear? I promise you. I love you."

Grandma Naomi slumped, her body finally relaxing. "I love you, too, kid."

Anthony eased her into a chair, then gestured for Devin to come forward. "Hey, I got a surprise for you. It's Devin!"

Grandma Naomi smiled at him. "Devin . . ."

Anthony quietly told Devin, "It's okay. She's fine now. It passed. This happens; it's just part of it. I need you to stay with her now while I talk to her doctor."

"Just, like, alone?" Devin squeaked.

"She's your grandma," Anthony said. "She won't bite. She might fart." He paused. "Okay, she *will* fart."

As soon as Anthony was gone, Grandma turned to Devin and said, "Stink. Do you know where my video camera is? Matty took it."

"I'm Devin, Grandma."

A nurse stepped into the room and gave Devin a free pass to leave. "It's okay, honey," she told him. "I've got her from here."

Back out in the hallway, Devin sidled up to his dad, who had just wrapped up a conversation with one of the doctors. "What is that?" Devin asked Anthony, pointing to the plastic bag.

"Matty's hoodie from that night," Anthony said. "Mom petitioned to get it back. And they finally gave it to her, after thirty years." He glanced at his son. "She could never accept he was gone. Matty was her favorite." He paused. "You know he was your age when he died? You really remind me of him."

"Really?" Devin muttered. "I thought he had everything going for him?"

"He did," Anthony smiled. "He was the best. Just like you. He made bad choices sometimes."

"Just like me?"

Anthony put his arm around his son's shoulders and pulled him close. "You guys came home pretty late last night. Did you have fun?"

"Yeah, I guess." Devin shrugged.

Anthony smiled. "Good, I guess."

By the time they got home, Devin's stomach was grumbling. "I'm starving. Turns out pudding and Ensure do not fill you up."

"Why don't you order from CJ?" Anthony suggested. "On second thought, it will take forever and half will be eaten. Maybe order us a pizza or whatever sounds good to you. Takeout menus are in one of those boxes." He held up the bag with the hoodie and moved toward the basement door. "I'm gonna go put this downstairs."

"Hey, Dad," Devin said, sensing his dad's sadness. "Are you okay?"

"I'm fine," Anthony promised. "I'll be back up in a few."

As soon as he got down to his workroom in the basement, Anthony took a seat on the stool at his table. Taking a deep breath, he unsealed the bag and removed Matty's hoodie from inside. Suddenly, he noticed a few tiny bits of dirt lodged into the fabric of the sweatshirt. He swung his desktop lamp over to get a closer look. "Strange . . ." he muttered, noting that the dirt wasn't dirt at all—but some kind of black spore.

Carefully, he scraped the spores off the fabric and sprinkled them into a petri dish, then placed it under his microscope. Under magnification, Anthony noted that the spores resembled a double helix. "What the hell is this?"

Back upstairs, Devin was paging through the box of menus when he came upon a photo album labeled *1994*. He opened it, flipping to a photo of his uncle—who looked exactly like the kid he'd nearly stumbled into inside the tunnel the previous night. The kid with black oozing from his eyes. That kid . . . was his dead uncle?

Devin pounded on the basement door, yelling out, "Dad!"

"In a minute, Devin," Anthony called back. He was watching the magnified spores move through a live feed on his computer. Just as Devin knocked, the spores began to pulsate.

Devin pounded again. "It's about Uncle Matty!"

Anthony was so transfixed by the scene he was watching on his screen that he didn't notice that the ferns on the shelf above had moved toward the petri dish. Slowly, they were consumed by the spores, and Anthony gasped as vine-like tendrils flew out from the petri dish at an alarming rate, causing him to fall off his stool. "Really not a good time, Devin!"

The vines continued to spread, engulfing the basement in seconds. Anthony grabbed for the dish under the microscope, which was obviously the origin point. But mere seconds after grabbing for the sample, the plant's tentacles began to wrap around his hands, binding them to the petri dish.

"I need to tell you something!" Devin hollered down through the door. "It's important!"

The vine-tentacles lunged, snaking toward the door, yanking Anthony off his feet as they tried to climb the stairs to get to Devin. "Devin!" Anthony screamed. "Do not come down here!"

The vines shot toward the door, slamming against it with a loud bang. Suddenly, Devin began to hear the same low hum he'd heard inside the tunnel the night before. He cupped his ears and staggered away, eager to get as far as possible from the sound.

As soon as Devin was gone, the vines reversed direction and shot down the stairs again. Leaving Anthony in their wake, they slithered along the basement floor and down through the drain in the middle of the floor.

Out on the street, Devin grabbed his phone and punched in his sister's number. "Pick up," he muttered. "C'mon, Cece, pick up!" Once again, the humming began. Devin spun around just in time to see the lid pop off a manhole cover in the middle of the street—and he watched, horrified, as vines crawled out of the opening and raced toward him. Before he could even scream, the vines had wrapped around Devin's shoulders, the force causing him to drop his phone. The vines lassoed him, then began dragging him backward across the pavement, tightening a little more each time he moved. Just before the vines sucked him into the sewer, Devin spotted Frankie down the block. "Frankie!" he screamed.

"Devin?" Frankie called out. She was pretty sure she'd heard Devin's voice calling out to her, but when she spun around, the street was empty.

"Help!" Devin cried from below, struggling against the vines that had him trapped underground. "Frankie! Help!"

Frankie looked around, puzzled, but then she shrugged and continued toward home.

Down in the sewer, Devin squirmed and writhed, finally managing to get one arm free just as the end of the vine pried his mouth open. The humming sound grew louder and Devin's eyes began to cry black tears just as the plant's tentacle extended toward his throat to consume him.

As he began to lose focus, Devin spotted the source of the vines: They were all connected to a root that was coming from some sort of drain in the wall, with a metal grate that had been propped open. Straining, Devin reached his free hand toward a broken, rusty pipe hanging from the sewer wall. The vine was inches from reaching down into his throat when Devin mustered up every last ounce of his energy and threw the pipe. It knocked the latch holding open the grate, and the door swung closed, slicing through the roots. The rest of the vine went slack against Devin's body.

Finally free, Devin crawled through the sewer, dragging himself up and out to the street again. As soon as he'd made it back to safety, he shook his head and looked around, confused. "How did I get here?"

Inside his basement lab, Anthony was utterly stumped. One moment, he'd been battling some exceedingly powerful vine-like tentacles, and the next, they'd stopped pulling and began a hasty retreat back into the petri dish he was holding in his hand. Heading toward his worktable, Anthony noticed that the petri dish under the microscope was now empty.

Absentmindedly, he scratched at the palm of his hand. It was red and raw from grasping the dish while wrestling with the vine. But as he scratched, the itching on his palm grew worse. He opened his hand and looked down, horrified to see that spores had imprinted on his skin. He unbuttoned his shirt cuff and rolled back his sleeve.

He let out a soft gasp. The spores had spread up and around his entire forearm.

"That's. Not. Good."

Meanwhile, inside Fort Jerome, footsteps echoed as someone walked purposely through the tunnel toward the old, abandoned bunker. A hand reached out to press a button on the wall. With a hiss, the hatch on the bunker's floor slid closed once again.

CHAPTER SIX

Anthony stayed down in the basement long into the night, eventually falling asleep at his workbench. But sometime in the middle of the night, he awoke with a start. There was some kind of tiny sprout growing out of his wrist, and it had begun to crawl up his arm and tickle his face.

He shot upright, suddenly wide awake. Tiny, beet-colored roots had sprouted from his skin and were now moving as if they were alive! For a moment, he was captivated—what *was* this strange, seemingly living plant growing out of his skin? But then he realized it was *his* skin and he gasped. "Gross, gross, gross!"

Tugging furiously at the roots, Anthony tried to extract whatever had burrowed into his arm. But the roots were deep, and as he tugged, the tendrils of plant growing out of his skin began to coil around his fingers as if they had a mind of their own.

Frantic, Anthony searched his desk for a tool that might help him with the task. He grabbed at a pair of pruning shears, grasped the roots between the two pincers, and then yanked. But nothing would give; the plant was buried deep inside his arm and was determined to stay there. "Ahhh!" Anthony screamed, suddenly noticing that the roots trailed all the way up his arm, where they were attached to something even bigger lodged under the skin of his forearm. "Oh, c'mon! What's *in* there?"

With no other choice, Anthony plunged the shears into his arm and tore the skin back, flesh peeling away as he reached in to try to grab the source of the roots: a red, flowerlike bulb covered in plant goo that had somehow sprouted *inside* his arm. The bulb seemed to be throbbing to the pulse of Anthony's own heartbeat.

Anthony wailed, realizing he'd become the host to some sort of mysterious, living plant *thing*. "I . . . don't . . . like . . . this!"

Frankie woke up and moaned, remembering the events at the fort the night of the party. Glancing at a picture of Trey in her bedroom, she closed her eyes and sighed. "I'm done with you, Trey," she vowed. "I don't ever want to see your face again."

She began to pull at the hundreds of photos of her and Trey that lined the walls of her bedroom. They had a history, sure, but she was pissed. She'd had enough of Trey and his controlling ways. Someone could have really been hurt thanks to his little stunt.

As soon as she was dressed in her work T-shirt, she headed toward her coffee shop job. Along the way, she passed Junior's Auto Body Repair, and there was Trey, scrolling through his phone, not paying attention to his dad's lesson in how to change a car's oil. "You hear me?" Joe Junior yelled to Trey from under the car. "Because too often I gotta clean up your idiotic messes."

Frankie watched as Trey's face went hard, bristling at his dad's criticism. But he brightened as soon as he saw Frankie stepping into the shop. "Babe!" he said with a big smile. "Hey."

"Can we talk?" Frankie asked seriously.

Trey smirked. "You're not still mad about the other night? Because it feels like it's past the statute of limitations."

Frankie shook her head. "Uh, yeah. I'm still mad. Devin was really freaked out."

"Yeah, he was," Trey laughed. "He was all, like, '*Uh, we don't have this in the city*.'" He put on a dopey voice to mock Devin.

"It wasn't funny. And you do stuff like this all the time. Why do you always have to mess with people? When you're like that, it makes me feel bad. Maybe we're not—"

Trey grew serious. "Not what?"

"Not, like, you know—" Frankie began.

"No, I actually don't," Trey cut in. "Look, did I go too far at the fort? I don't know. Maybe. Maybe not. I thought it was funny, but I get that you and your friend didn't. But the fact is I'm stressed out. I got a lot going on and it's hard for me to ask for support, but sometimes a guy needs it."

Frankie felt her resolve crumbling. She knew Trey needed her, and she loved that she was the person he leaned on. "I know, I hear that—"

Trey cut her off. "I mean, I do so much for you. All I do is think about you and try to be the man who deserves you. And then you come at me like this?"

"No," Frankie said, shaking her head. "I'm not 'coming at you'—I'm talking. I'm just talking."

"You know, Frankie," Trey said, his voice sharp, "sometimes you just make it so hard to be in this relationship."

"I'm sorry. I know you're trying," Frankie said, putting her hand on his arm comfortingly. "And I want to be supportive."

Trey huffed. "Then be supportive. I gotta get back to work."

Frankie smiled at him, trying to patch things over. "Okay. Will I see you later?"

"I don't know, Frankie," Trey said as he walked away. "I just don't know."

A few hours later, Frankie was sitting behind the counter at work, still thinking about their conversation. How was she always so good at messing things up between her and Trey? But she was pulled out of her own thoughts when Cece and Devin came through the coffee shop door in mid-conversation.

"That was extremely stressful in an already stressful situation," Cece was saying. "I mean, living with Dad for a whole summer would make anyone lose it. Your mind was playing tricks on you."

Devin shrugged. "I guess."

"Devin," Cece said, leveling her twin with a serious stare. "Promise me that you'll keep this between us. You can't tell Dad."

"Hey, guys," Frankie said, alerting them to her presence.

Cece studied the menu and beverage case, then asked, "Where's the kombucha?"

"We just ran out," Frankie answered dryly.

"Oh. When's your next shipment?"

"Never," Frankie told her. "Like an A rating, it's something this coffee shop won't ever get. *But* we do have coffee."

"Yoo-hoo's brown," Devin announced, holding up a bottle. "It must have the same stuff in it as kombucha."

"No," Cece groaned, then spun toward the door. "A thousand times no. I gotta get to debate camp. See you guys later."

"So, what do you want?" Frankie asked Devin.

He grinned and teased, "I'll have a half-caf double skim macchiato."

Frankie hid her smile. "Shoot, we just ran out." Devin laughed. "*But* if you help me set up the furniture outside, I can get you a regular coffee with recently expired half-and-half."

"This is not a very good coffee shop," Devin said, then headed outside to start setting up the furniture with Frankie.

Once they'd finished, she brought him his promised free coffee and said, "Hey, I'm sorry about the other night. Trey can be a lot, but he's really been working on himself. Well, he downloaded a meditation app. But blowing the transformer was over the line."

Devin shrugged. "It's okay."

"It isn't. It wasn't."

"It doesn't matter," Devin said. "Because that wasn't the scariest thing that's happened to me lately."

"Okay," Frankie said, eyebrows lifted. "I'm listening."

Devin suddenly remembered his sister telling him they should keep what happened the night before between them, a secret. He quickly said, "Never mind, it's nothing."

"That sounds like something."

"I didn't see anything."

"So . . . you saw something," Frankie said, curious. "Tell me what you saw."

"Okay," Devin said, eager to offload on someone other than

his sister. "This is gonna sound strange, but . . . I wrestled some kind of vine thing. In the sewer."

"Like, a *plant* vine?"

"I guess?" Devin said, throwing his hands up. "But they weren't any plants I've ever seen, and my dad's a botanist." He glanced at Frankie, wondering if he'd lost her yet. "Next you're going to say I'm losing my mind and I'm imagining it all."

"That's not what I was going to say. What I was *going* to say is, that's really creepy. Believe weirdos."

Devin smiled at her gratefully. "Thanks. Cece thinks I imagined it all."

"Why would she?"

"Well, when we were younger I used to have these 'waking nightmares.' They were super vivid. Cece's probably right, and that's all it was."

Frankie gave him a sympathetic look. "Either way, it sounds like a rough night. Did you talk to your dad about it?"

Devin rolled his eyes. "My dad's been in the basement all night."

"He does spend a lot of time down there."

"How do you know?"

Frankie laughed. "I mean, what else is there to do out here in Gravesend except be in each other's business?"

CHAPTER SEVEN

A nthony was ready for medical warfare. He dipped a cotton ball into rubbing alcohol, then wiped the skin around the pulsing plant bulb. It stung—a lot. And what he was about to do was going to sting even more. But he didn't have a choice. He had to get this plant *thing* out of his arm.

Gritting his teeth, he took a spading fork and wedged it between his arm and the base of the bulb. Then he hit record on his phone, since he had a feeling he was going to want video evidence of what was about to happen. "I have what seems to be a bulb or tuber of some unknown species attached to my forearm via its roots," he said into the camera lens. "I will now attempt removal via spading fork. My hope is that by turning this into a purely scientific experience, I can reduce my deep, deep fear of what is actually going on." He took a breath, then said, "Nope, not working."

Then with a quick countdown to steel his nerves, Anthony plunged the gardening tool into his arm and yanked at the bulb as if it were an ordinary garden weed. With a twist of the tool, the bulb pulled away from his arm, and Anthony could see roots underneath it, still attached to his skin. The roots held fast as he tugged—until they finally gave way, and Anthony extricated the bulb from his arm.

He placed the specimen and his tools down on his worktable, then turned to the camera again. "Removal of bulb-slash-tuber has been successful. And deeply unsettling." Dripping with sweat, Anthony plopped down on his stool and studied the red, bulblike plant.

What on earth had he just dug up?

During his lunch break, Trey headed over to visit his girl at work. But as he got close to the coffee shop, he slowed his pace when he spotted Devin exiting the building. He stopped short when he saw Frankie lean in and give him a hug before returning inside.

Trey didn't like this; he didn't like this one little bit. That was *his* girl. Trey pushed open the front door of the café. "Hey, baby," he said.

Trey leaned in for a hug just as Frankie asked, "To what do I owe the pleasure—"

"Love," Trey said quickly. "I'm a man full of love. Isn't that a good enough reason for a visit?"

"Of course—"

Trey kissed her, then gave her a quick squeeze on her waist. Frankie bristled and squirmed. "Ah!"

"What, you ticklish?"

Frankie laughed uncomfortably. "Yeah, I don't like that."

He kept squeezing.

"Stop," Frankie repeated, still laughing. "Seriously."

He continued to squeeze, ignoring her request altogether.

"I said *stop*," Frankie snapped. She pushed him into a rack of potato chips, sending the bags everywhere.

"Now look what you've done," Trey chided.

"What is wrong with you?"

"No, what is wrong with *you*, Frankie?" Trey shouted. "I saw him."

"Who? Devin? Is this seriously about Devin? He was just getting a coffee."

"Plus a big hug from the world's friendliest barista?"

"Trey, forget Devin. C'mon, you came over for lunch. You want a sandwich or something?"

Trey shrugged, then grinned. "You know me better than anyone." As Frankie made his sandwich, Trey asked, "So, what were you and that loser talking about?"

"I can't," she said quickly. "I promised I wouldn't tell anyone."

"C'mon, I'm your boyfriend. We're a team. We don't keep secrets from each other."

Frankie considered this, well aware she couldn't risk making him any angrier. With a sigh, she relented. "Okay, but just don't tell anyone . . ."

In his basement workroom, Anthony had called one of his colleagues, Patti, for help figuring out what had been growing out of his arm. "I need to identify the exact species of this plant," he told her, hoping that their combined years of research at NYU would help them solve this mystery together.

"Yeah, well, that's the thing," Patti began, gazing seriously from Anthony's monitor during their FaceTime call. "These photomicrographs you sent me aren't plant-based."

"Of course they are," Anthony said, taking another look under his microscope. "I just took them. It's a plant."

"It's definitely not a plant."

"Well, what is it, then?"

"It's an animal," Patti told him. "And it's carnivorous." Anthony's mouth dropped open as Patti went on. "Where did this sample even come from?"

Anthony quickly said, "Thanks for your help," then ended the call. Suddenly, he had an idea. He stood up, headed upstairs, and hopped in his car.

Later that afternoon, Trey was heading out of work, flush with an idea of his own. "Hey, I'm going to cut out for the day, Pops. Can I take the Olds tonight?"

Joe Junior tossed his son the keys, then warned him, "Don't block that Plant Dick's driveway. That nerd's the last thing I need to deal with. You listening to me?"

"Yep!" Trey lied. "Got it."

He hustled home, parking the Olds right in front of Anthony's empty driveway—blocking the Plant Dick's entrance. He got out of the car and grinned, then stepped up to Anthony's front door and knocked.

"Hey," Trey said when Devin answered the door.

"What's up?" Devin asked, a confused expression on his face.

"I know exactly what you're doing," Trey said ominously. "You make up some insane story about vines attacking you so you can get with Frankie."

"Sh-she's my friend," Devin stammered. "And I told her that in confidence!"

"You don't get to have 'confidence' with my girlfriend."

Just then, Frankie stepped out of the front door of her own house down the street. She'd heard the commotion and was worried about what Trey might be up to now.

"Frankie," Devin said as she came toward them. "You told him? I trusted you."

"You shouldn't have," Trey scoffed. Then he pulled back and threw a punch at Devin. He lifted his chin and strode away, proud that he'd made his point. "That's right."

Devin recoiled from the surprise punch, and Frankie gasped, frozen where she stood. But as soon as Devin had recovered, he ran quickly down the porch stairs, tackling Trey from behind.

Frankie closed the distance between them as the two guys began to wrestle. She tried to get closer so she could pull them apart, but they were moving too fast. "Stop it! Trey, come on," she cried from the sidelines.

"What?" Trey asked, finally breaking away from Devin, his

breath coming in quick bursts. "You worried I'm going to hurt your new boyfriend?"

"Trey. That's nuts," Frankie assured him. "Nothing is going on between us."

"Just stay away from her," Trey told Devin, sticking a finger inches from his face.

"Or what? You'll give me a green neck with your fake Chrome Hearts chain?"

Trey lunged for Devin again, but Frankie grabbed his arm before he could land another hit. "It's not fake!" he growled. "My aunt got it for me in LA!"

"Go home, Trey," Frankie ordered. "Now!"

As soon as Trey had stormed off, Devin hustled inside. Frankie trailed after him, quickly heading toward the freezer to get some peas to put on his swollen face. "I can't believe you told Trey," Devin said, accepting the frozen bag from her. He winced as he placed them over the spot where Trey's punch had landed.

"I'm sorry. He's my boyfriend. I tell him everything."

"Why would you want to date a guy like that?"

Frankie scoffed. "Oh, you're going to blow in here for the summer and judge me."

"For dating that psycho? Yeah."

"He's my best friend," Frankie said softly, settling into a chair across from Devin. "He's my safety net. He's my rock—"

"Or at least as dumb as one."

"Look. My mom works all the time," Frankie explained. "She doesn't own a condo in the Village. I don't have my dad anymore.

And I don't have anyone to catch me if I fall. I turn eighteen and it's all on me. *You* turn eighteen and you get, like, a trip to Europe."

Devin listened, understanding that his life was a whole lot different than Frankie's. He shrugged. "It's actually the Bahamas," he said with a small smile. "But yeah, I see what you're saying."

"You don't know anything about me," Frankie said softly. "Or at least nothing that you haven't learned by stalking my TikTok." She stood up and headed for the door.

Devin chased after her. "You said that wasn't weird—"

"Well, it is. It's super-duper weird."

"Your meathead boyfriend just sucker punched me in the face for *talking* to you. And you're mad at *me*? What is happening? Is the world upside down? Is this the *Real Housewives of Gravesend*?"

"I'll see you later, Devin," Frankie said, walking off the porch and crossing the street to her own house.

Devin headed back inside, slamming the door behind him. He couldn't help but wonder, *Exactly how many things are going to go wrong for me this summer?*

CHAPTER EIGHT

When Anthony returned home later that afternoon, he found Joe Junior's Oldsmobile parked—once again—in front of his driveway. "You've *got* to be kidding me!" Glancing across the street, he noticed Trey hanging out on his front porch. "Trey! Can you move your car?"

Trey wanted nothing *less* than to help Devin's dad. He was still furious and worked up from the fight earlier that day. "In a minute," he called back. "Go water a cactus or something."

Anthony flung open his car door. He was on his last nerve after everything that had happened since the previous night. He hustled around to his trunk and popped it open, grabbing a tire iron from inside. He then marched over to the Oldsmobile and slammed the tool into the car's driver's side window.

"Yo!" Trey screamed. "What are you doing?"

"Since you seem unable to move your vehicle, I'm doing it for you, my friend!"

"Are you out of your mind?"

Anthony reached through the shattered window and shifted the car into neutral. Then he pushed it away from his driveway, clearing the path for his own car. "I am not. This is, unfortunately, the only remaining logical solution." He slid back into his car and pulled into his cleared driveway.

Trey raced across the street, still screaming. "What the hell? My dad is going to kill me!"

Anthony stepped out of his parked car and shrugged. "That sounds like a *you* problem." He hustled inside, and the first thing he saw was his son in the kitchen with a bag of frozen peas on his face. "What happened?"

"Don't worry about it," Devin muttered.

"Are you sure?" Anthony asked, glancing quickly at the basement door.

Despite the evidence that *something* was clearly going on, Devin could tell his dad was distracted by whatever he was working on downstairs. He sighed. Devin didn't want to get in the way of what was important to his dad—and not telling him about the fight meant that he couldn't get mad about it. "Yeah, one hundred percent. I just tripped and fell. No big deal."

"Okay, well, if you're okay, then I think I might go—"

"—in the basement," Devin finished for him.

"Right," Anthony said with a nod. "It's gonna be a great summer, right after this. What I'm working on down there right now is going to change everything, Devin. It's big. It's really big. I just need a little time." He opened the door to his workroom and slipped inside, closing and locking the door behind him.

At the bottom of the stairs, Anthony hustled toward his desk. He opened the shopping bag he'd brought home and pulled out a small box with holes in the sides. Flipping it open, he reached in and grabbed a live mouse before turning to the bulb that was sitting right where he'd left it in the center of his desk. "Let's see how carnivorous you really are," he muttered, and he dangled the mouse over the bulb.

Nothing happened. Anthony shook his head. "This is silly."

But just as he was about to put the mouse back in its box, the bulb began to unfurl, slowly, like a flower. But its slow movements didn't last long. Suddenly, it shot upright and consumed the mouse whole, like a snake striking its prey.

Anthony jumped back, startled, then leaned in to watch as the bulb slowly closed back up again. The bulb shuddered and began to morph—into the shape of the mouse it had just devoured. "Okay, all right," Anthony muttered. "That was a thing that just happened." He gingerly picked up the mouse-shaped bulb by the "tail" and placed it carefully inside the large basement freezer. He had some more experiments to run.

When Anthony came upstairs a few minutes later, it was immediately obvious to Devin that something strange was going on with his dad. He was acting even odder than usual—and that was not a low bar. "Dad, is everything okay?"

"Do you remember the petting zoo in Sheepshead Bay I used to take you guys out to?" Anthony asked, out of the blue.

"With Fuzz Lightyear the alpaca?"

Anthony nodded. "What do you think they do with the old animals there?"

"Wow," Devin said with a laugh. "I always thought I'd have this conversation when I was older."

Anthony chuckled. "I just need some meat—"

"Have you tried the butcher?" Devin cut in.

"Duh!" Anthony rapped himself on the head. "I should have thought of that." He raced out the door.

Devin watched him go, wondering what on earth was happening inside his dad's head. "I'm definitely not imagining things," he mused. "Because stuff is getting weird around here. Including me talking to myself."

Less than an hour later, Devin opened the door to accept his food delivery from CJ.

"Here are all your egg rolls," CJ said, thrusting a bag toward him.

Devin grinned at him. "See, I feel like you shouldn't say 'all your egg rolls.' That just increases suspicion that you ate one of them."

"And yet, I did not," CJ vowed.

"You and I both know you did. You can have them. That's not why I called you. I need your help."

CJ pulled out an egg roll and began to munch on Devin's food. "With what?" he asked through a full mouth.

"I need to prove something to myself."

As Frankie walked toward Junior's Auto Body Repair shop, she could hear Trey's dad yelling from almost a block away. "I told you not to park there!" he was screaming at his son. "And you did it, anyway. This is on you. Why are you always so dumb? What's wrong with you? Maybe if it comes out of your paycheck, you'll remember to listen next time."

Joe Junior stormed out of the repair shop, nearly colliding with Frankie as she made her way inside.

"I can't believe that guy!" Trey growled as soon as he saw her.

"You did block his driveway," she pointed out.

"Oh, so now you're taking his side. I thought we were a team."

"We are," Frankie reassured him. "I'm not taking sides, I'm just pointing out that you were at least, like, a little bit at fault."

"Here's the thing: I wasn't at fault, like, at all. I had literally parked the car for, like, a second—and then Nerd Dad smashed my window. That's his fault, and his whole family needs to learn a lesson."

"Trey!" Frankie cried as Trey stormed off. "Trey!" She chased after him, catching up just as he reached Anthony's yard.

"I'm going in," Trey growled.

"Do not do this, Trey," Frankie warned. "You could get in big trouble."

"It's self-defense."

"No, this is *trespassing* and vandalism and breaking and entering and basically everything other than self-defense."

Trey poked around the edge of the house, grinning when he noticed the basement window. "Oh, look—an open window."

"Where?" Frankie asked. Trey grabbed a rock and smashed it through the window. Frankie groaned. "You can add property damage to that list."

Trey spun around to face her. "If you're not going to support me, why don't you just go home?"

"It's not support, it's being an accessory," Frankie said with a hiss. She knew she couldn't be a part of whatever revenge scheme Trey had planned. This was on him.

As Frankie walked away, Trey lowered himself through the shattered window into Anthony's basement. He dropped onto the large chest freezer, landing with a thump. Hopping to the floor, he looked around the space, marveling at all the shelves of hydroponic plants. "What a freak," he muttered to himself. "Nerd Dad's growing himself some weed." Striding quickly across the basement, Trey made his way directly to the shelf full of plants nestled under grow lights. He leaned in close and tipped the shelf, watching as it slammed to the floor. "Oops."

One by one, Trey tipped over every single tray of plants, clearing whole shelves as he tore a path of destruction through Anthony's treasured basement lab. Trey moved faster and with more purpose at each new shelf. When he finally reached the far corner of the room, he grabbed at the whole shelving system and, with all his strength, managed to tip the entire wall of plants over in one satisfying smash. The shelf broke on impact with the floor; UV lights shattered into glistening shards across the basement. Plants and dirt were scattered everywhere.

Laughing hysterically, Trey backed away from the scene. He leaned against the freezer and took in his work. "Mess with the Olds, you get the horns." He pulled out his phone and took a selfie, his middle finger up and evidence of his actions visible behind him.

As he took shot after shot, capturing the whole basement in photographic detail, Trey was too distracted to notice the freezer door hinging open . . . until it was too late.

Hearing the creak of the door, Trey finally glanced behind him. When he looked down into the open freezer, he let out a scream just as the *thing* hidden inside reached out to grab him. Before Trey could do anything to stop it, the creature had dragged him into the frozen coffin—then slammed it closed again to seal him away inside.

CHAPTER NINE

Devin led CJ to the manhole where he'd been dragged underground by rogue vines the previous night. CJ helped him lift open the cover, all while reading aloud from his phone: "'It is unlawful for any person not otherwise specifically authorized by law to remove, or cause to be removed, a manhole cover from a public sewer'—"

"I am aware of the legalities," Devin said, cutting him off.

"You asked me to hold a flashlight," CJ reminded him. "This is not just holding a flashlight."

"Don't worry. I'll take all the blame," Devin promised.

"That's not how the law works." As they slid the manhole cover off to the side, Devin slipped down through the opening and gestured for CJ to follow him.

"Can't this wait until the morning when it's full daylight and not, like, a huge scary bummer?" CJ begged.

"You promised."

CJ shook his head and followed Devin beneath the street. Below, Devin splashed onto the sewer floor, but CJ stalled out on the ladder before jumping down. "I'm not going any farther." He aimed his flashlight at the wet ground, and then let the light trail after Devin as he retraced his steps from the previous night, poking into the water. "You know that's toilet water from all of Gravesend, right? You're sticking your hands in the waste of a thousand flushes."

"Just aim the flashlight," Devin instructed.

"They test toilet water to see what diseases are spreading in our community. You're basically standing in measles."

"So?" Devin asked.

CJ said, "My hope is that if I keep talking, I won't throw up. It's part of my process."

Devin searched through the water, pulling up remnants of the vines that had wrapped around him and nearly choked him to death the night before. Now, they looked like seaweed covered in sludge. "I wasn't imagining it," he said, holding the vine clusters up in victory. "Look at this."

"Congratulations," CJ said dryly. "You found dirty, dead plants. I bet if you keep fishing around, you'll find some dead rats, too."

"There's a few over there," Devin said, pointing.

"Where?" CJ shrieked. He swung his light in the direction Devin had pointed, then swung it back again. "I just realized I don't actually want to see dead rats."

A few blocks away, Frankie was fretting inside her house. Trey had been down in Anthony's basement for over an hour, and she was getting worried. She looked out her window but saw no sign of him. She pulled out her phone and texted him: *Are you still in there? XOXO.* But before giving him a chance to respond, she called him, only for it to go straight to voice mail.

Frankie's anxiety got the best of her, and before long, she

grabbed her jacket and headed out to investigate. Once she was standing outside the Brewers' broken window, she leaned over and yelled inside, "Trey! Trey, you down there?" There was no response. "It's been ages! You better get out of there!"

She paused, listening for any sound of movement. Nothing. Frankie released a deep sigh, removed her jacket, and draped it over the broken window ledge to lower herself into the basement. *So much for not being an accessory*, she thought.

Once Frankie had softly dropped to the ground inside the basement, she looked around. There was no sign of Trey, but evidence of his visit was everywhere. "What did you do?" she whispered into the empty mess of a space, surveying the destruction.

She pulled out her phone and dialed Trey's number again. This time, she could hear it ringing. Spinning around, she searched for where the sound was coming from. *There!* Right at the base of the freezer. "Trey . . ." Frankie said, walking toward his phone and picking it up. Now she was really nervous—what had happened down here? And where was Trey?

She shoved a phone into each back pocket and stepped onto the freezer to help her climb out of the window. But even standing on the freezer, she realized she was too short to pull herself up and out to street level.

Frankie let out a deep sigh. She didn't have a choice—she'd have to exit through the main house. Heading for the stairs, Frankie climbed up—only to find the basement door locked from the outside. She was stuck.

Before she could figure out her next steps, Frankie heard the sound of the freezer door slam closed behind her. Frankie spun around. "Babe? Is that you?" Walking back toward the freezer, Frankie shivered. The basement was creepy, and now she was hearing noises. She opened the freezer door cautiously, but there was nothing inside—it was totally empty. "Trey," she said, her voice shaking. "This isn't funny. I'm serious. Where are you?"

Suddenly, Frankie felt something grab her shoulder. She screamed and turned, scrabbling for freedom—but when Frankie saw what had her captured in its grip, she lost all hope. The hand of some kind of living plant *monster* was holding her fast. She opened her mouth to scream again, but then she saw something that made her pause: Trey's chain was hanging around the creature's neck. "Trey?" she whispered.

The plant beast opened its mouth to try to respond, but it could only make horrible guttural noises, no words. Unable to speak, the monster—*Trey?*—grew frustrated and started lashing out at the shelving surrounding it. With a mighty pull, the monster heaved a nearby shelf violently, sending it crashing toward the ground. And Frankie was standing right there, ready to break its fall.

From deep inside the sewer, arms filled with dead vines, Devin suddenly stopped moving and looked up at the open manhole cover. "I think I just heard someone scream," he told CJ.

"Okay, now I'm done here," CJ said, totally freaked out. "Possessed vines, sewers, dead rats, and now screaming? Nah. I hereby retire from flashlight-holding duties."

He climbed quickly back up the ladder and took a relieved breath of fresh nighttime air at the surface, Devin right behind him, dragging a few of the vines in his wake. Devin hopped on the back of CJ's electric scooter, and together they drove down the block toward the Brewer house. "What smells so bad?" CJ asked. "It's us, isn't it?"

Devin shrugged, even though his friend couldn't see him. "We were in a sewer."

When they pulled in front of Devin's house moments later, CJ left the engine running. "Good luck with whatever you're looking for," CJ told him. "And know this: I will never help you again." Then he took off as Devin dragged armloads of dead vines toward his house.

As soon as he got up to the porch, Devin began to open the front door—but a second later, something slammed against it from the other side. *Bang!*

Devin startled as the thud came again. *Bang!*

As he started to step backward, the door suddenly burst open with a loud *craaaack!* It hit Devin hard, sending him flying off the porch and over the railing into the bushes, the vines flying from his arms. Devin lay there for a moment, trying to catch his breath. And when he finally looked up, he questioned if he was seeing things.

Because there was some kind of monster storming down the middle of the road away from the house, holding Frankie over its shoulder like a helpless prisoner.

Devin wailed as he hustled to his feet. "Frankie!"

CHAPTER TEN

Anthony pulled into his driveway not long afterward, lugging an enormous goat carcass out of his trunk in a bloody sack. As he dragged it across the lawn, a woman walked by with her dog, and the dog growled. "Yes, it's a dead goat," he told the alarmed woman with a friendly wave.

Inside, he hustled toward the basement steps and dragged his treasure down the stairs. "Oh no," he muttered as soon as he saw the mess that was his lab. "What happened?!" He turned and screamed up the stairs, "Devin!"

Suddenly, his laptop began to ring with an incoming FaceTime call. Anthony hustled over and answered, quickly blurting out, "Patti, I'm a little preoccupied at the moment—"

"I ran your research by a few colleagues," Patti told him. "We think you're onto something big here."

"Was I right?" Anthony asked, excited. "Is it a new species?"

"Definitely. Like Nobel Prize level. You need to bring in the specimen so we can verify the results."

"Uh, yeah," Anthony said, glancing toward the freezer. "Okay." He raced over to the freezer and flung open the lid. It was empty except for a pile of crumpled clothes. "Oh no. No, no, no."

"Anthony," Patti's voice rang out from his laptop. "You still have it, right?"

He lifted the sweatshirt out of the freezer and inspected it. It read *Junior's Auto Body Repair* on the front: *Trey's* shirt. "I, uh . . . I'm gonna call you back."

"Is everything okay—"

Anthony slammed the laptop closed, ending the call. "This is not good."

The street outside Junior's Auto Body Repair was silent and still. Inside, Frankie had just come to, and now the events of the past half hour were all coming back to her: the Brewers' basement, finding Trey's phone, the *creature*. She looked around, trying to figure out where she was. *The shop*, she realized with a sigh of almost relief. The Oldsmobile was eight feet off the ground on a hydraulic lift, and a single light shone from somewhere inside the office.

Suddenly, the plant monster—*Trey?*—came into view inside the garage and made its way toward Frankie, holding a metal object of some kind. She jumped out of her chair and scrambled backward, terrified and unsure what the creature was capable of. "Whatever happened to you in that basement," she told the Trey-monster, "we can fix. We just need to call someone. Get you some help. Okay? Will you let me do that? Trey, will you let me do that?" The monster continued toward her, holding the object out. When it got closer, Frankie could see that it was a paint scraper. The creature handed it to her, and Frankie looked at it with confusion. "What do you want me to do?"

The Trey-monster gestured along its arms and Frankie furrowed her brows. "You want me to scrape the stuff off you?" The monster nodded, pulling her hand along its body to signal for her to start scraping right away. "Okay, Trey. I'll try."

It turned around so she could start on its back. Wincing, Frankie pressed the metal scraper where its shoulder blade would be and began to scrape a layer of plant material away. Again and again she repeated the gesture, knowing full well how much it must hurt to have a layer of your skin—or whatever it was—peeled away. But no matter how much she scraped, the layers didn't end. "Trey," she said, "it's not coming off. It's all plant stuff."

The Trey-monster stepped away from her, moving to a small mirror to see for itself. Growing agitated, it began to scratch violently at the plant material, trying to pull it off its own limbs.

"Calm down," Frankie warned the creature. "It's going to be okay. We'll figure this out." She put her hand gently on its shoulder.

Suddenly, Devin's voice rang through the still air. "Frankie? Frankie!"

As soon as they saw Devin approaching the shop, the Trey-monster grew more agitated. It began to shake, its entire body morphing into the embodiment of living, breathing rage. Knocking Frankie's arm away from its shoulder, the Trey-monster turned its attention to Devin instead, ready to take out all the frustration on Trey's nemesis. The creature moved to the garage's entrance, blocking Devin from getting any closer to Frankie.

Picking up a piece of pipe from the floor, Devin moved toward the Trey-monster. "Get away from her!" He swung the pipe, but the weapon was no match for the beast.

The Trey-monster grabbed Devin and swung him up onto the hood of the Oldsmobile as if he were nothing more than a stuffed animal. Devin slid off the car's hood and rolled onto the hard ground below, battered and bruised. The monster stood over him, menacing and alarmingly angry. Leaning down, the Trey-monster wrapped its hand around Devin's neck and lifted him into the air.

Devin dangled, helpless, as the Trey-monster choked him. Just as Devin sucked in what he was sure would be his last breath, Frankie gently reached forward and touched the beast's shoulder again. "Baby," she cooed. "It's okay. You're my boyfriend. We're a team. Forget about him. He doesn't mean anything."

The Trey-monster slowly released Devin, letting him fall to the ground where he choked and gasped for air. "C'mon, baby," Frankie continued. "Let's go back to the garage so I can support you on whatever this journey is." She led the creature back inside the garage as Devin staggered to his feet.

"Frankie," Devin cried out. "What are you doing? Run away!"

She turned to look at him. "Devin, go home." She reached up and pulled down the steel rolling door, trapping herself inside the garage with the plant monster who'd somehow consumed Trey. Slowly, Frankie coaxed the Trey-monster under the Oldsmobile, gently whispering, "Right here, Trey."

It hesitated, but then did as she asked.

"I just want you to stand over the drain," she told the monster, pointing at the drain on the garage floor, right underneath the suspended car. "I'm going to get the power washer. We'll wash all this stuff off of you. Okay?"

The Trey-monster stared at her, then nodded. Frankie walked quickly toward the power washer, but at the last second, she moved toward the switch that controlled the hydraulic lift instead. "I'm sorry, but I have to do this." Just as the Trey-monster realized she'd deceived him, Frankie flipped the switch—and sent the Oldsmobile crashing down to the garage floor at full speed.

Splat!

A few moments later, Frankie took a deep breath and rolled the garage door back up. Devin was still trying to get in to help her. He saw the look on her face and pulled her in for a hug. "Are you okay? What was that thing?"

"Trey—I think," she murmured into his arm.

Devin looked over Frankie's shoulder and saw the mess of plant monster muck that had splatted across the garage floor. It trailed out from under the car like an oil spill. "Oh my god," he said quietly. "Gross." Then he realized how bad this was. "Let's get out of here." He grabbed Frankie's hand, and together they raced away.

As soon as Frankie and Devin were out of sight, there was a stir of movement from the darkness in the empty garage. The mud and gloop of plant mess beneath the car began to congeal into a mass that crawled up and into the underbelly of the Oldsmobile. Once it had disappeared into the bowels of the car, the engine revved to life, the motor hummed, and the broken car window fused back together as if it had never been broken at all.

CHAPTER ELEVEN

The next morning, Devin woke up feeling like he'd been hit by a ton of bricks in the night. And in a way, that's kind of what happened. He still couldn't believe he'd faced that plant monster and survived—and gotten Frankie out of its clutches alive, too. He slumped down the stairs, each step a twinge to his sore body, and his dad greeted him with a quick, "Hey, have you seen Trey?"

Devin stopped in his tracks. His dad was fiddling with some tools as he tried to fix the basement door, which had been broken during the plant monster's escape. *What did his dad know about what had happened?* Playing it cool, Devin said, "Good morning to you, too."

"Good morning," Anthony said, distracted. "I'm sorry. I just need to talk to Trey."

"Have you tried our driveway?" Devin suggested, injecting some lightness into his shaky voice.

"I don't think he'll be parking there anytime soon."

Cece came down the stairs just then and asked, "Who?"

"Trey. Have you seen him?" Anthony glanced up from his repair work.

"Why would I have seen him?" Cece scoffed.

"I don't know," Anthony said. "Kids see kids."

81

"Okay, well," Devin said with a forced-casual shrug. "I'll keep an eye out for other kids. I gotta run."

"Where?" Cece asked.

"I told Frankie I would meet her."

Cece grinned at him. "I knew only a girl could get you out of bed this early."

As soon as he'd gone, Anthony gestured toward the kitchen and said, "Oh, Cec, that kombucha I made you is ready."

"Really?" She followed her dad into the kitchen, eagerly accepting the jug full of brown gloop. "Super gross!" she said happily as she poured a large serving into her travel cup.

"Do you think Dev is okay?" Anthony asked his daughter. "He seemed pretty distracted this morning."

Cece paused. She didn't really want to say anything—twin code—but she knew she should probably tell her dad about what had happened to Devin, at least in a roundabout way. "Honestly, Devin's been acting a little weird. He said that his memory has been a little fuzzy."

"Fuzzy?"

"He said the other night he thought he fell into the sewer or was pulled down or something—"

"Why didn't he tell me this?" Anthony asked urgently.

"He didn't want to scare you and make you think what was happening to Grandma was happening to him."

"No," Anthony said. "That's not possible—" He cut off, suddenly connecting some of the dots for himself. "Did Devin go down into the basement? When the door was open?"

Cece looked at him, realizing her dad was turning this into a work thing again. "What does that have to do with anything?"

"Just tell me, Cece."

"Of course. I'm trying to talk to you about something serious that's going on with Devin and all you want to talk about is your work in the stupid basement."

"No, that's not it—"

Cece grabbed her cup and rushed to the door. "It's fine. I'm late. Thanks for the kombucha."

CHAPTER TWELVE

One year ago, Alex's life had changed dramatically—for the worse. She'd been at a party in an abandoned house when the house caught fire. Unfortunately for Alex, when the cops caught up to her after she fled the scene, there were fireworks in her backpack. Which meant all signs pointed to *Alex* as the bad guy.

Only she knew who was really to blame . . . and it wasn't her.

When the cops had handcuffed her and put her in the back of a squad car, she did the one thing she hated doing more than anything else (because it almost never worked): She begged her mom for mercy. "Mom, please," she pleaded from the backseat of the cop car. "You have to get me out of this. It wasn't my fault."

Alex's mom, Jen, had held up the backpack full of fireworks and gave her daughter a look. "Don't. I'm not here as your mother right now. I'm a detective. And this is a crime scene. You're the prime suspect. Officer Morales is going to come talk to you, but I would advise you not to say anything else."

"But you believe me, right?" Alex had urged, wishing her mom could just be her *mom* sometimes and not always such a cop. Her mom's silence was all the answer Alex needed. As Jen turned and strode away, Alex had tried one last time to call for her help. "Mom! Mom!"

Ever since then, she'd been trying to get her mom to believe she wasn't guilty of arson. That she wasn't as bad as her mom thought she was. That she was worth loving.

And now, her mom was settled into the living room alongside Alex and her probation officer, Teresa, to hear what was up next in her mandated punishment. "Coming off your six-month sentence in the juvenile correction facility, you are now entering into a probationary period where your actions will be monitored by the department. Do you understand?" Teresa leveled Alex with a serious look, making sure she fully grasped the consequences of further incidents.

"Yes," Jen said, glancing in her daughter's direction.

"It needs to come from her," Teresa said pointedly. Alex nodded. "I need verbal acknowledgment."

"Yes," Alex said.

"You can't leave the state without permission," Teresa went on. "You can't commit any new crimes—which should be obvious, but bears repeating—and it's very important that you avoid harmful and disreputable places and people."

Alex muttered, "I thought you said I couldn't leave New York."

"Alex," Jen warned. "Don't."

Sliding paperwork and some kind of device across the table, Teresa said, "The Department of Probation is issuing you this ankle monitor as an electronic tagging device. You must sign here to agree to the terms and conditions."

Jen gave Alex a look, and Alex leaned in to sign the form.

Teresa locked the ankle monitor onto Alex and then continued, "Alex's future success is going to be a family effort. Follow the rules, continue your community service, and keep to your curfew—ten p.m.—or you will find yourself back in front of a judge and, in all likelihood, back in custody." She brushed her hands together and said, "Okay, that's it."

As soon as Teresa had gathered her things, Jen stood up and said, "I'll walk you out."

"Thanks for stopping by, Teresa!" Alex chirped. She tucked the ankle monitor under her sock, checked her lipstick, and slung a backpack over her shoulder.

"Where are you going?" Jen asked, coming back into the living room.

"I've got some bodies to bury." She grinned at her mom, then grew serious again. "I have community service."

"Alex," Jen called after her. "Take this seriously or I can't help you."

Alex bristled, remembering the day she'd been caught—red-handed—and her mom hadn't believed her. She'd trusted everyone else before trusting her own daughter. "Well, you didn't help me in the first place, so that's nothing new."

Jen sighed. "Just stay out of trouble."

Alex went to her community service, dutifully wearing the ugly orange vest they forced on them so everyone knew to stare when they passed by. As she stabbed a piece of trash, Alex caught sight of someone she'd been looking for ever since the night of that awful party over a year before. "Hey, Murph!" she called out to the guy slinking out the front door of the deli across the street.

Glancing over, Murphy quickly unlatched his bike lock so he could flee.

Alex chased after him, but before she could get more than a few steps, a supervisor caught her by the shoulder. "Hey, where do you think you're going?"

"I need to talk to that guy," Alex said. Murphy knew *exactly* who was responsible for that fire, and she wanted to talk to him to clear some things up.

"Take one more step and I'll happily write you up," the officer told her. "Three more write-ups and I get a gift card to Carrabba's Italian Grill. Which I love."

Alex resumed her trash pickup duties, glaring at Murphy as he rode off to freedom on his bike.

While Alex did her community service, Jen headed off to work. Today's first stop: Anthony's house. Stepping down the stairs to his wrecked basement, Jen whistled. "How do you know it was Trey who did this?" she asked Anthony, who'd called to file a complaint.

Anthony held up a work shirt with *Trey* embroidered on the front. "Why would he leave his clothes?" Jen asked.

"I think this was some kind of retaliation," Anthony said with a shrug. "That kid has problems."

"Retaliation for what?"

Anthony confessed, "I kind of smashed his car window."

"Anthony!"

"He was blocking *my* driveway!"

"Why would you do that? I told you not to mess with them."

"Don't blame the victim, Jen. Trey took something very valuable and I need it back."

Jen glanced at Anthony's laptop and other equipment, all of which was still in place. "What was of more value than your laptop and all this high-tech equipment?"

"My research," Anthony said. "And he doesn't realize that it is very"—he paused, realizing he couldn't exactly say *dangerous* without inviting more questions—"unstable and fragile."

"Well, now this is all making a lot more sense. So you want to file a police report?"

Anthony shook his head. "No, I just need to get my research back. As soon as possible."

Jen sighed. "Okay, let's go find him."

Jen and Anthony headed over to Joe Junior's shop, hoping to find Trey. "Hey, Joe," Jen called out. "Got a sec?"

"Oh, good," Joe Junior said, glaring at Anthony. "I was just gonna call you about that guy. He's a menace."

"I was just moving the car," Anthony shot back. "Trey keeps—"

"Anthony, let me handle this." Jen put a hand on his arm.

"Look at this, Jen," Joe Junior said, pointing to the Oldsmobile. "Look what this monster did to my—" He stopped in front of the driver's side window and noticed the glass was good as new again. "I guess Trey already fixed it?"

"Great," Jen said. "One problem solved. Now I need to talk to Trey. Is he around?"

Joe Junior put up his hands, defensive. "Not if he's in some kinda trouble."

"He's in *big* trouble," Anthony blurted.

"Anthony—" Jen warned.

"He has something of mine," Anthony said.

"Is Trey here?" Jen asked.

"Not yet," Joe Junior said. "He takes Frankie to work and then hits the gym—benches two hundred. What's going on here?"

"It's not a big deal—" Jen said, trying to keep things calm.

Anthony looked at her in horror. "Um, yeah—it is."

"Don't worry about it," Jen told Joe Junior. "I'm handling it. We'll check in with Frankie. But just have Trey call me as soon as he gets in."

As he and Jen walked out, Anthony suddenly noticed something lying on the ground—Trey's silver chain. He picked it up and put it in his pocket before anyone else noticed.

The second they'd left the shop, Joe Junior dialed his son's number, but the phone went straight to voice mail. "Trey," he growled, leaving a message. "What did you do now? Call me."

Once her community service shift was over, Alex hustled back into her regular clothes, sloughing off the orange vest as fast as possible. She waited on the corner for CJ, who she'd called to meet her.

"Hey," CJ said, rolling up on his scooter a few minutes later.

"Can you lend me your scooter for, like, a few hours?" Alex asked without introduction.

"Oh, let me think about that . . . *no.*"

"C'mon, CJ. This is important."

"Look, I'm a food delivery professional. Not the friendly neighborhood task rabbit. I've already ruined a pair of kicks helping Devin walk through a river of toilet water."

"Toilet water?" Alex said, raising an eyebrow. "Now I have some questions."

"I'm done," CJ said, revving the scooter's motor. "I'm tapped out on 'helping.' You want a lift? Call Lyft. Or ask Trey." He pointed down the street toward Joe Junior's shop, then rode off, leaving Alex without a set of wheels.

As she strode toward the shop, Alex dialed Trey's number. "C'mon, Trey . . ." she whispered, urging him to pick up. But it went to voice mail. Alex watched as one of the shop's mechanics moved the Oldsmobile out of the garage and parked it on the street, keys tucked away under the visor. Quickly, Alex left a message on Trey's voice mail. "Heeeeey, you know how we're best friends and always doing each other favors? I need to borrow your car. Quick errand. Call me back in the next minute if that's a problem."

She hung up, then glanced quickly around to see if anyone was watching. Coast clear, she hopped into the driver's seat. Alex took the keys out from under the visor and started up the car. Just as she shifted into drive and pulled out of the parking spot, a tiny spot of black goo bubbled up around the parking brake, then receded back into the car's floorboard before Alex had a chance to notice it at all.

CHAPTER THIRTEEN

"Cece!" Alex hollered through the open driver's side window, trying to stop the other girl before she headed down into the subway.

Cece took a sip of her kombucha, spinning around to see who'd called her name. When she saw Alex, her eyes narrowed. "What are you doing in Trey's car?"

"Driving. He's letting me borrow it." She paused, then asked, "What are you doing right now?"

"Heading into the city. I've got to present my argument against free speech at debate camp today."

"Okay, fascist," Alex said with a smirk. Then she added, "Ditch it."

"We can't all be bad girls."

"I'm going to assume you mean 'bad girls' in a hot way and not a judgy way."

Cece held back a smile. "One should never assume."

"Cute. Look, I need you to help me out with something."

"I told you," Cece reminded her. "I'm going to debate."

"Not today."

"Excuse me?"

"Please. I don't want to have to say anything."

Cece stiffened. "Say anything about what?"

"Um, you boosting lip gloss at the pharmacy."

"Nice try. But no one is going to believe you over me."

"You're right," Alex said, reaching for her phone. She held it out to show Cece the video she'd taken at the pharmacy. "But they'll believe this." She grinned at Cece, knowing she'd won. "Hop in!"

Meanwhile, inside the coffee shop, Frankie couldn't think about work—all she could think about was what had happened to Trey the previous night. And what she'd done. "How is this happening?" she asked Devin as soon as her only customer had left the shop. She switched to a whisper. "I killed him. I killed Trey!"

"No. No, you killed a monster that looked sort of like Trey. And had the same bad taste in jewelry."

"That is not making me feel better," Frankie said with a groan.

"It was not him," Devin said. "And you had no choice. He—*it* was trying to kill *me*."

"What are we going to do?"

"Maybe we should tell my dad."

"What? No!" Frankie gasped, horrified. "I am like a walking true-crime podcast. I was the last person to see him alive."

"Okay, okay. But whatever happened to Trey started in my dad's basement . . ."

"Well, then, maybe he's like the *last* person we should talk to." Just as Frankie said that, the shop door swung open and Alex's mom walked inside. She was wearing her work clothes and was obviously on duty as a detective. Frankie felt her face go hot.

"Hey, Frankie," Jen said casually.

"Good morning, Detective."

"Hi! Hello, top of the day," Devin chimed in. "I'm Devin."

"Devin . . ." Jen said, recognizing him as Anthony's son. "I haven't seen you in a long, long time."

"Yeah, it's been a while. I bet I look older."

Jen quickly switched topics and turned back to Frankie. "Um, hey, have you heard from Trey today?"

"No, I haven't," Frankie said quickly.

"He didn't bring you here this morning?"

"No," Frankie said, searching for an excuse. "Uh, we kind of got into a fight last night."

"Before or after he went into Devin's dad's basement?" Jen asked.

Frankie and Devin exchanged a look, which Jen immediately picked up on. "Before," Frankie said. "Devin told me about that. Crazy."

Jen nodded. "Then you know it's important that I talk to Trey. Just let me know if you hear from him." She handed Frankie her card and left the shop.

A short while later, Alex pulled Trey's Oldsmobile over in front of a pizzeria. She told Cece her plan: "All you have to do is go in there and ask the guy working behind the counter where his buddy Murph is."

"And why can't *you* do this?"

"Because he doesn't want to talk to me, and his friends know it."

Cece studied her. "Okay, well, I'm not gonna do that. And you can't force me to, because I have new information on you." She tapped her phone and said, "On our drive over here I learned a few things on the old phone here—thanks, Google—and it turns out if you're on probation and you get reported for *anything*, like stealing a car, for instance, you go right back inside. There's even this nifty anonymous number you can call to report someone."

"I *borrowed* the car," Alex repeated.

"You might want to workshop that before the police come."

Alex sighed heavily, realizing she was going to have to change tactics if she wanted to win Cece over. "Okay, look, I really do need your help. Everyone thinks I started this big fire last year. That's why I went away to juvie. But I didn't—"

"Why do they think you did, then?"

"I mean, I've dabbled in some 'light criming.' Truancy . . . vandalism . . . larceny . . . I stole a vending machine and rolled it off a pier to impress a girl. Which is somehow considered grand theft auto because of the wheels?"

Cece laughed.

Alex went on, "Burning down a house is not on my Essentials playlist. I went to juvie for something I didn't do."

"Okay, so I'm not saying I believe you, but if you didn't burn down a house, who did?"

"Murph!" Alex said forcefully. "I just need you to help me find out where he is so I can get him to confess."

"So you can turn him in?" Cece asked. She believed Alex but didn't know why this was so important to her.

"No, I'm not a snitch," Alex said quickly. "It's so I can prove it to my mom."

Cece studied her and realized how much Alex was hurting. She smiled gently, then said, "You know, you could have just started with that." Then she hopped out of the car and strode into the pizzeria.

Alex lurked inside the car, trying to crane her neck to see if she could make out what was happening in the shop. Suddenly, the old CD player inside the car began to play; Alex looked at it, confused. She flipped a switch to turn it off, but nothing happened—the music kept playing.

A moment later, the heat came on inside the car at full blast. She fiddled with the dials, trying to turn it down, but the heat just kept blowing, stronger and hotter. It was as if the car had a mind of its own. She was about to fling open the door to escape the relentless heat when Cece appeared at her window, and suddenly both the heat and music shut off. Alex caught her breath, realizing she'd been starting to panic, and rolled down her window.

"I got Murph's work address," Cece said with a proud smile. She raced around and hopped in on the passenger side. "Oh my god, it's so hot in here."

Alex put the car in drive and pulled into traffic, thinking, *That was weird*.

CHAPTER FOURTEEN

Jen was back at the precinct trying to make sense of things. Her coworker, Officer Morales, bent over her desk and gestured to the file she was reviewing. "The 1994 missing teen case?" he asked, curious.

"Yeah," Jen said with a sigh. "There was a break-in at Fort Jerome, where it happened. Just got me thinking."

"You knew them, right?" Officer Morales asked her.

Before Jen could answer, she noticed Joe Junior rushing across the office toward her. "Joe! Did you bring Trey in?"

"No, I can't find him," Joe Junior told her, his face serious. "He still hasn't come to work. He's not answering his phone. He hasn't been to see Frankie. And I had my guy park the Olds on the street and now it's missing."

"The car is missing?" Jen asked.

"At first, I thought it was just Trey being Trey, and I was, like, I'm going to kill this kid—in a manner of speaking," Joe Junior told her. "But now I'm starting to get worried."

Jen grabbed her keys and stepped away from her desk. "Don't worry. I'll find him. Morales, let's get an APB out now."

Alex pulled up in front of the address where Murph's friend had told Cece he was working. They watched as he helped an elderly man into a chair, noticing Murph was wearing scrubs. "That's him," Alex said, pointing.

"He's a home health aide?"

"I guess so . . ."

"I'm not really getting 'lying arsonist' from him. You sure you have the right guy?"

"I'm sure," Alex said, then popped out of the car. She crossed the street, beelining for Murph, who was now unlocking his bike nearby. "Hey! Murph! Sorry to interrupt your date. We need to talk."

Murph backed away. "Alex . . . hey."

"I spent six months in detention for you and I didn't snitch."

"You brought the fireworks," Murph reminded her.

This was true. But Alex had her counterargument. "*You* set them off inside."

"Fair."

"So I want you to do something for me."

"Yeah?" Murph asked, immediately suspicious. "What's that?"

"Tell my mom the truth."

"Your mom, the *cop*?" Murph said, sneering.

"Off the record," Alex assured him.

Murph popped his bike lock open. "Okay, yeah. Of course. All you had to do was ask. I owe you one." Then he hopped on his bike and took off, full speed.

"Murph!" Alex screamed after him, running back to the Oldsmobile. He had a head start, but she had wheels, too. She quickly started the car, stepped on the gas, and peeled out into the street.

"Whoa! What are you doing?" Cece asked, bracing herself as the car swerved through traffic.

"Chasing him," Alex deadpanned.

Cece held on for dear life as Alex raced the Olds after Murph, growing ever closer with each second. "If you're trying to scare the guy, I think he's sufficiently scared."

"Good," Alex said, nudging their speed up another notch.

"Then can you please slow down?"

Alex glanced over at Cece and saw that she was seriously freaked out. Something in her softened and she nodded. "Fine."

She eased her foot up off the gas. But as soon as she did, a small tendril of black goo emerged from the car's floorboard and wrapped around her leg. It pulled her foot back down, increasing the speed even more.

Moments later, the Oldsmobile's headlights began to glow. The car gunned forward, the engine roaring as they gained even more speed and drew ever closer to the back of Murph's bike. Murph spun around and screamed, "Alex, what the hell?"

"You're going to run him over!" Cece yelled.

Alex glanced down at her foot, which was very obviously pinned to the gas pedal. "I'm not trying to! I can't move my foot. It's stuck on the gas."

"What are you talking about?"

Alex frantically tried to pull her foot up, but the car kept getting faster and faster. They were moving in, closer and closer, and Murph was mere inches from the Oldsmobile's front grille. They could see the sweat pouring off him and the terrorized look on his face when he turned around to glance back at them.

"You're gonna kill him!" Cece screamed. "Stop!"

It was Alex's turn to be totally freaked out. "I'm not doing anything!" She continued to pull at her foot, but it was trapped in place.

Just before the front of the car nudged Murph's back tire, Cece reached over and grabbed the steering wheel. With a crank, she pulled them off course and avoided crashing into Murph—but soared straight into a lamppost instead.

Smash! The car wrapped around the pole, finally coming to a stop. On impact, tiny black spores flew out of the vent in the dashboard. Neither Cece nor Alex noticed when several of the spores settled into Cece's kombucha, taking up residence inside her beloved travel cup.

"Are you okay?" Alex asked, turning to check on Cece.

Cece was staring at the cracked windshield, in shock. "I can't believe I fell for it," she said, hastily unbuckling her seat belt. "The innocent routine. You really are messed up."

"It wasn't me!" Alex protested.

"Sure," Cece said with a harsh laugh. "Just like it wasn't you who burned down the house."

"It wasn't!" Alex watched, helpless, as Cece threw open the passenger door and got out of the smashed car. "How are you going to get home?"

"I would rather take my chances with the world's sketchiest rideshare driver!" Cece slammed the door closed and marched away.

Alex got out of the car to inspect the damage. Trey was going to *kill* her; the front bumper and hood were both crushed inward, and the headlights shattered. The car was toast. She got back into the driver's seat and tried to start it. No dice. Looking around, she realized she was totally alone. The street was empty, and there was no one to ask for help. Then she noticed Cece had forgotten her nasty kombucha cup. She leaned out the window and called after her, "Hey! You left your kombucha!" But Cece was too far away to hear her. With a sigh, Alex put the travel cup in her backpack's side pocket and muttered, "Great. Just great."

She hit the dash in frustration, wondering—not for the first time—how she always managed to mess up absolutely everything.

CHAPTER FIFTEEN

Anthony climbed down into the sewer, searching for some answers of his own. He couldn't stop thinking about what Cece had told him about Devin, and he wanted to know why his son had been down here. Reaching into the murky water on the ground, Anthony pulled up a clump of dead vines. They were exactly like the vines he'd wrestled with in his basement a few nights ago. "Where did these come from?" he wondered aloud.

He followed the trail of vines down one end of the tunnel. They stopped near a grate, and Anthony realized exactly where it led: "The basement." He clutched a collection of the vines in his hand and hustled back toward the surface and home, eager to examine them further.

Once he was safely back in his lab, Anthony delicately scraped pieces of his sample specimen into a petri dish. Then he covered the dish with another piece of glass and wrapped the whole thing carefully with tape, making sure nothing could escape from his sample. He flicked on his camera, recording the whole process as he began the test.

"I think the spores from Matty's hoodie are the cause of everything," he said, speaking directly into the camera. "The vines that grew from the petri dish seem to have potentially traveled farther than was known to me—doing unknown damage. They also grew the bulb in my arm. And while I do not know where the bulb currently is—the spores seem to." Anthony picked up the dish and moved around the room, watching with great interest as the spores moved inside the petri dish. They almost acted like a little compass, congregating together on one side, as if pointing in the direction they wanted him to move.

"You want to go somewhere, don't you?" he cooed to his sample. "Let's go find out where."

Alex was still trying desperately to start the car. She had to get home; she'd finished community service hours ago, and her mom was going to start freaking out about where she was. Not because she cared—but because she didn't trust her. "C'mon," she begged the car. "Work with me, baby. We just gotta get home . . ." Her phone rang, and the caller ID read *Officer Mom*. Alex shook her head and muttered, "Nope."

A text followed a second later. *Staying out of trouble?* her mom had asked.

Alex ignored the text and tried the key again, but the car was obviously not going anywhere. Just then, she began to hear a low hum, followed by the sound of twisting metal. She got out of the car and walked around to the front. The fender was bending back into shape. Moments later, the windshield cracks began to heal themselves, and the hood smoothed itself out and locked back into place—good as new.

The car revved to life. Alex stepped backward, confused. "How did it do that?"

Looking around, Alex realized she didn't have much choice but to get into the car, unless she wanted to be stranded out here in the middle of nowhere. She slid into the driver's seat and leaned across to grab her phone off the passenger seat. Before she'd even closed the door, the car jolted and lurched backward. The sudden jerk caused Alex to drop her phone onto the ground outside.

The engine let out a monstrous roar as the car peeled out onto the street, slamming the driver's side door and trapping Alex inside with no way to call for help.

Shortly afterward, the cops showed up at the scene after hearing reports of a crashed Oldsmobile. They found the downed power lines and crushed lamppost on the scene, but there was no damaged car in sight.

"Any idea what happened here?" Jen asked Officer Morales and his partner. When she heard it was an Oldsmobile that had crashed, she'd rushed over, hoping to finally find Trey.

"No," Officer Morales answered with a shrug. "Someone driving by called it in."

"And it was definitely the Olds?"

Officer Morales nodded. "Matched the description of Trey's car perfectly. But there's no trace of the car, no shattered glass, no paint on the pole, not even a hubcap."

Jen shook her head. "You can't just hit a lamppost like this and drive away."

"Nope," Officer Morales said. "It doesn't make sense."

Jen sighed. "Well, Trey knows how to fix cars." She was worried. This was all so bizarre. Thinking about Trey being missing made her worry about Alex. She pulled out her phone to call her daughter, but as soon as she'd dialed, she heard the faint sound of Alex's ringtone coming from somewhere nearby. She scanned the scene and spotted the ringing phone near the curb. Jen bent down and picked it up, noticing that the cracked screen read *Officer Mom*.

She glanced again at the busted lamppost, then back at her daughter's phone. Was her daughter in that car? And if so, where was she now? Under her breath she muttered, "Alex, I hope you're okay, because I swear . . . you're grounded until you're forty." Then she silenced her daughter's phone and stuffed it in her pocket.

Back on Jamaica Bay Road, Alex was very much not okay. The Oldsmobile was driving down the road at breakneck speed, and Alex was *not* the one controlling things in the driver's seat. She stomped on the brake pedal, trying hard to overpower the car, but it seemed to be driving itself. "C'mon, c'mon! Stop!" She looked up toward the sky and begged, "Please, I'll be good, I won't jaywalk or even share my Netflix password, I promise. I swear! Just *stop*!"

She pulled up the emergency brake up and the car fishtailed, but a moment later, it righted itself and continued on, even faster now. "What is going *on*?" Alex screamed. Suddenly, she noticed another car on her tail. It was Murph! "Murph!" Alex screamed. "Help me! This car is possessed or something!"

Murph's car picked up speed, and he raced alongside her, trying to cut her off. Alex could tell he was trying to race, but she was terrified about what the Oldsmobile was capable of. She screamed out the window, "I'm not controlling the car!"

As soon as he saw her free hands and panicked expression, Murph's anger shifted to confusion, then fear. Distracted, he lost control of his car and veered off the road, delivering him to a better fate than Alex's. She couldn't do anything other than hold on as the Olds twisted away from the road and crashed through a security gate—onto a dirt road that led directly into the bay. A wall of large rocks loomed ahead of her, the final cliff before she and the car would plunge downward to Alex's certain death. "No!" Alex screamed. She was trapped in a deathmobile that was about to sail off a ledge and into the water below.

Across the bay, Alex could see the old Fort Jerome looming, large and imposing. "I'm gonna die, I'm gonna die," Alex muttered, trying to kick and pound at the driver's side door. It was sealed tight and wouldn't budge. Grabbing her backpack, Alex scrambled into the backseat. Searching quickly, she found the lever that brought the backseat down and flicked it open. She wriggled her way into the trunk, then grabbed at Trey's bolt cutters. "Yes!" Using them as a battering ram, Alex smashed at the latch inside the trunk, over and over, until it popped open. She squatted, ready to pounce, and waited until the perfect moment. Swinging her backpack around to the front so it could serve as a sort of protective padding during the fall, she leaped out of the Oldsmobile's trunk just as the car flew off the jetty and crashed into the water far below.

Alex landed on the ground, rolling to a stop. "Ow," she muttered as the pain from the impact hit. "That's gonna bruise . . . everywhere." Limping, she slowly walked to the edge of the rock jetty and looked down just in time to see the car sink beneath the surface and disappear underwater. "Nobody's gonna believe this . . ."

Slowly and painfully, Alex turned and made her way toward home. Her ankle monitor blinked yellow, on and off, searching for a signal.

She'd been walking for what felt like miles when Alex heard a car pull in behind her. For a moment, panic set in as she worried that the Oldsmobile had somehow found her again. But when she turned, she saw it was her mom's car—and for the first time in ages, she was relieved to see her familiar face. Until her mom screamed, "What the hell, Alex?"

"I'm not even going to try to explain it to you," Alex grumbled.

Jen looked around, trying to figure out what her daughter could possibly have been doing out here in the middle of nowhere. "It's almost ten. You know what that means."

Alex sighed. "Just drive me home. Or back to juvie. I don't care. I'm gonna miss curfew, anyway."

Jen glanced at the dashboard clock, which read 9:53. "You

haven't missed curfew yet." She slammed on the gas, flicking her lights and siren on to clear the road. They made it home with seconds to spare, and Alex's ankle monitor blinked green to show she was in the clear. Alex offered her mom a smile—it felt good to know she really *did* have her back when she truly needed it.

"We need to talk about Trey," Jen said, warming up some leftovers for Alex's dinner.

"Why?"

"I need you to tell me where he is."

"I don't know." Alex shrugged.

"You were in his car, Alex."

Alex cringed. "I borrowed it . . . kind of. I left him a message and took it. Why? What's going on with Trey?" She glanced at her mom and noticed just how worried she suddenly looked. "Mom, what happened to Trey?"

Jen gave her a serious look. "I don't know."

Inside Fort Jerome, Anthony walked quickly through the tunnels and made his way to the old control room—the last place he'd seen his brother alive. Glancing down at the petri dish full of vine spores he held in his hand, Anthony saw that they had finally calmed down; this was obviously where they had been leading him. Suddenly, the spores began to spread out in the dish, slowly forming a strange geometric pattern.

"Matty," Anthony whispered, "what happened in here?" He

panned his flashlight over the old, rusted equipment. Suddenly, his light caught a human form hunched over in the corner of the room. Anthony gasped as the person lunged at him. He staggered backward, then righted himself when he realized who it was: Trey!

Reaching forward, he took the teen's arm. Trey followed willingly as Anthony led him through the tunnels, back outside. He wrapped his jacket around him, but Trey said nothing—just stared, silent, as if he was in some kind of shock. As soon as they got back to Anthony's car, he dialed Jen's number. "I found Trey," he told her.

"Where?" Jen asked.

"Jen," Anthony said, his heart racing. He didn't answer her question; instead, he simply said, "It's happening again."

CHAPTER SIXTEEN

No one knew it, but Cece had not gotten into debate camp. She'd spent her entire life creating an image—the ideal image of the overachieving success story—but this summer's rejection from her prestigious, dream debate camp had nearly shattered everything.

Her best friends, Harper, Aisha, and Iris, all had their lives together and were each doing amazing and important internships and research fellowships this summer. But Cece? Cece was faking it. She was a total fraud. Not only had she not gotten into debate camp, she was also lying about the need to take the subway into the city every day. The whole situation had her feeling like her twin brother, who seemed to have little to no aspirations in life at all.

And if Cece wasn't good enough for debate camp, that meant she wasn't good enough, period. Her debate coach had assured her this wasn't the end of the world. But to Cece it was, and the rejection had sent her spiraling into weeks of anxiety and stress. The only silver lining was that she had managed to fool everyone into thinking she *was* someone who was still good enough.

As she ate her breakfast at the dining room table in her dad's house, dressed and ready for her day at "debate camp," she listened to a voice mail her mom left her earlier that morning: "Remember, you have your alumni interview with Ms. Bosco this afternoon. I know you're taking a break from debate camp for this, but it's totally worth it. Just make sure your coach understands how important this is or you wouldn't miss camp. I know you're doing that already." Her mom took a breath, then launched back into her voice mail monologue. "Okay, I'm totally stressing you out, honey. You're so perfect, you're already, like, five chess moves ahead of me on this stuff. Good luck at the interview. I love you."

Cece rolled her eyes. "Like I would forget the most important thing happening all summer." She glanced at her phone calendar, which had only one thing listed on her schedule: *ALUMNI INTERVIEW*. This was it—her only shot—and she was paranoid she was going to blow it.

Anthony walked into the kitchen just as Cece was about to leave. "Hey," he said. "I really wanted to drive you to the Village for your interview today, but I want to go check on Trey—"

"I thought you hated him?" Cece interrupted.

Anthony cringed. "That's harsh. I still want him to be okay. Devin already left to meet Frankie at the hospital. He texted me. It's just all a little crazy—"

Cece shrugged. "I get it. It's totally fine."

"I just know it's really important—"

"Dad. It's not a big deal."

"I know that you know that I know that this is a big deal and that you are pretending it's not a big deal in order to reduce your stress level about this big deal."

With a smile, Cece asked her dad, "You're my therapist now?"

"I'm sure you'll nail it, Cece," Anthony said confidently.

Cece was a lot less confident. But she was good at faking it and had a reputation to uphold, so she said, "Of course I'll nail it. I nail everything. That's kind of my whole thing if you haven't noticed."

"No, I have noticed."

She flashed him a bright smile, glad that at least she was good at this one thing—fooling people into believing she was as good as she was always pretending to be. "Thank you. Okay, I should get going."

"Don't forget your stun gun!" Anthony called out as Cece headed for the door.

Cece pulled her stun gun out of her bag and held it up, calling back, "Just in case the interview goes south!"

As Alex headed out for her morning community service shift, her mom asked, "Where are you going?"

She held up her orange vest and retorted, "Prom."

Jen smiled, but it quickly faded as worry took over. "Look, I want you to be careful today."

"Careful? What are you talking about?"

"There's just some weird stuff going on," Jen said with a sigh.

Alex was intrigued; how much did her mom know about what was going on in Gravesend? "Can you be more specific than 'weird stuff,' Detective?"

"Want to be more specific about what happened with Trey's car?" Jen pressed. Alex just stared back, refusing to answer. She wanted to talk to Cece first. Jen sighed again. "Okay, then for now just listen to me and be careful. I'm going to swing by the hospital. Why don't you meet me there after your community service?"

"It's okay," Alex told her. "I'm good."

"Let me rephrase that. Meet me at the hospital after your community service. Please, Alex. This isn't because I don't trust you. It's because of . . ."

"Weird stuff?"

"Yeah. Weird stuff."

Alex shrugged and nodded. "Okay." She grabbed Cece's kombucha cup that she'd forgotten in the Olds the previous day, then headed for the door. She knew Cece's morning route by now, so she hustled to catch up with her new friend as she headed toward the subway into the city. She figured Cece probably didn't want to see her after everything that had happened the previous day, but Alex wanted to return her cup and try to explain what had happened. Even if she really *couldn't* explain anything at all.

But the second Cece spotted Alex, she picked up her pace, walking quickly toward the subway entrance. "Wait, Cece! I want to explain—" she called out, trying to get the other girl to stop and talk for a second.

"Are you here to finish me off?" Cece asked, finally coming to a halt on the sidewalk.

"No," Alex said quickly. "You left this behind yesterday." She held up the travel mug, then hastily added, "And I wanted to talk to you about, you know, what happened . . ."

"I do not have time for your flirty bad-girl chaos energy," Cece snapped. "And your flagrant disregard for public safety."

"Cece, please. I don't even know how to explain what that was."

"Your attire explains it for you," Cece said, pointing to Alex's orange vest and ankle monitor.

"I'm sorry, but it wasn't my fault," Alex said.

"You should get that tattooed," Cece muttered. "It's kinda your catchphrase. Look, as good as this non-apology is, I have to go. I have a crucial interview for my *future* to get to. I know that's not something you think that much about, but I can't have any . . . distractions." She spun and walked away.

"Hey," Alex called after her. She held up the kombucha cup, which Cece still hadn't taken from her. With a huff, Cece turned around again, quickly grabbing the cup before entering the train station. Neither of the girls had noticed that Cece's cup was sprinkled with black spores from the previous day's car ride. And if they had looked closely, they would have seen the spores wriggling . . . almost as if they were alive.

At the hospital, Trey was motionless under a fleece blanket, hooked up to an IV. His eyes were open, but they stared off into the distance, totally vacant. Frankie was sitting by his bedside, but she'd slumped over, fast asleep.

"Hey," Devin said, calling out to her softly as he entered the room carrying two coffees. She didn't stir. Devin tried again, louder this time. "Hey." Then Devin leaned in close to Trey's face and whispered, "Hello?" Trey blinked, causing Devin to startle and jump back into a tower of equipment.

The noise stirred Frankie awake. She straightened and said, "Sorry, I didn't realize I fell asleep."

"Yeah," Devin said gently. "You were so peaceful. I was trying to be quiet, but then you woke up on your own. I brought you this." He passed her one of the cups of coffee.

Frankie studied it and said, "You went to my café."

"Only the most average for you."

"Aww," Frankie said, grinning. "And lukewarm, just like we always serve it."

"And this," Devin said, passing her a bag of knitting stuff. "I figured you might need something to manage your stress." He sat down and asked, "How's he doing? Any updates?"

"No. He still hasn't said a word, or responded to anything, really. The doctor says he's in shock from whatever happened."

"How are you holding up?"

Frankie shook her head. "I'm just so relieved that Trey's still alive. But what's going on? We saw your dad leave the basement with that dish thing, and then he found him—"

"Naked," Devin finished for her. "I know. He, like, carried Trey naked out of that tunnel."

"And that's not even the strangest part. I mean, how did he find him?"

"He said it all had to do with my Uncle Matty's hoodie. Which doesn't make any sense." Trey sighed, and they both spun to look at him. "Maybe we should go for a walk," Devin said, suddenly worried that Trey was listening to their conversation.

Not long after they exited the room, Jen and Anthony arrived separately at the hospital. Both were eager to do a little investigating of their own. "Anthony!" Jen said, noticing him heading toward Trey's room. "What are you doing here?"

"We need to figure out what's going on," Anthony answered. "Get some answers from Trey."

"I can't let you do that," Jen said, stopping him before he could go any closer to Trey's hospital room. "You are a suspect here."

"A suspect? C'mon. What are you going to do? Arrest me?"

Jen sighed. She knew Anthony wasn't going to back down. "Fine. Just not one word when you're in there. And wait for a second while I scope things out."

"Of course," Anthony said, hands raised innocently. "You're the boss."

Jen walked into the hospital room and found Trey's whole family gathered around his bedside. "Have you found out anything yet?" Joe Junior asked Jen.

"Not yet. But I'm going to get to the bottom of it, I promise,"

Jen told him. "Listen, I need to talk to the doctor alone for a few minutes."

"Okay," Joe Junior said, leading his family toward the door.

As soon as they were gone, Jen ushered Anthony inside the hospital room. "Remember," she cautioned him. "I do the talking." Anthony didn't reply. She gave him a stern look and said, "Anthony!"

He shrugged. "You said not to talk!"

She rolled her eyes, then approached the doctor. "Hi, Doctor. I'm Detective Diaz. NYPD. I'm investigating the disappearance and, well, reappearance of Trey Jiminez." She glanced over, noticing Trey was still fast asleep in his bed. "What's his current state?"

The doctor, who was wearing plain clothes under her white coat, said, "Trey is displaying all the hallmark signs of PTSD, specifically acute stress disorder. He is aware of everything that is happening around him but just can't process it, if that makes sense."

Jen nodded. "Do you have any idea when he might start talking again? I've got a lot of questions to ask him. And we need to assess if there is a threat out there."

The doctor sighed. "He has traumatic mutism, and with cases like this, there's really no timetable. It could be hours, days, weeks, years."

"Years?" Jen asked. "Really?"

The doctor nodded. "I wouldn't get your hopes up."

Anthony piped up then and said, "I'm sorry to interrupt, but did you find any physical damage to his body? Or any growths? Bulblike—"

Jen cut him off, saying, "Anthony. Remember our deal?"

"Is this your partner?" the doctor said, studying Anthony carefully.

"No," Anthony said. "Just a concerned botanist."

"Then, I should go," the doctor said, hustling out of the room.

"Anthony!" Jen scolded as soon as she'd left. "Bulbs? What was that? You can't do that." She raced toward the hospital room door and stepped out into the hall, searching for the doctor. But she was already long gone.

In fact, the "doctor" she'd been speaking with had already shed her white lab coat, tossed it into a trash can, and hustled out of the hospital altogether, her boots clacking on the linoleum floor.

While Jen was looking for the doctor, Anthony took his chance to try to speak with Trey on his own. "Trey," he said, leaning close to his hospital bed. "It's Anthony. Hi. Sorry we were on bad terms when we last spoke. Do you mind if I just look at your arm real quick? I am a doctor, technically. I mean, not the kind of doctor who should be doing human medical stuff. Not that it's stopped me." He lifted up Trey's arm but quickly dropped it when the hospital door swung open and Devin and Frankie returned. "Dev! What are you doing here?"

Devin looked at his dad curiously. "Just keeping Frankie company. What are *you* doing here?"

"Keeping Jen company," Anthony stammered.

A nurse entered then and looked at the strange collection of people in Trey's room. "Are any of you family? Because if not, you need to go. This isn't a private karaoke room."

As they headed toward the waiting area down the hall, Jen returned and grabbed Anthony's arm. "I'm going to talk to your dad for a minute," she told Devin.

Devin leaned in toward Frankie as the two of them continued down the hall. "My dad was, like, inspecting Trey's arm."

Frankie whispered back, "Do you—do you think he's been experimenting on Trey?"

"I can't believe I'm saying this," Devin said softly, "but . . . maybe."

As soon as the kids were out of earshot, Jen got in Anthony's face and said, "Anthony. Go home."

"I'm just trying to help," he protested.

"I thought you could be discreet," Jen said. "But I was wrong apparently. If Joe Junior sees you here, he'll kill you."

"Jen," Anthony said urgently. "This is bigger than Joe Junior."

"What do you mean?"

"When you gave me Matty's hoodie back, I found something on it."

"What?"

"I found, like, a residual substance and I put it under my microscope, and it grew." Anthony paused. "It attacked me. And maybe Devin. And I think Trey."

"What?" Jen scoffed. "That's impossible."

"It's not just any plant. You're not listening."

"I *am* listening. You're not making any sense." Jen switched into detective mode. "Do I need to call a doctor for you to talk to?"

"No," Anthony assured her. "I don't need to talk to anyone. I'll just take care of it myself, like I should have done thirty years ago."

CHAPTER SEVENTEEN

W hen she got into the city, Cece headed toward the office
building where she'd be having her college alumni interview. She didn't feel confident. Instead, her head was jam-packed
with all kinds of worries and doubts, and she could feel her perfectly
crafted image crumbling with each empty summer day that passed.

She stepped into a coffee shop, hoping a quick dose of kombucha would help her regain her strength and focus. "Kombucha refill,
please," she said when she got up to the register. "I have my own cup."

Cece passed her travel mug to the barista just as she heard a
familiar voice behind her call out, "Cece?"

She spun around and saw that her three best friends—Aisha, Iris,
and Harper—were all sitting together at a nearby table. "OMG!" she
said, faking excitement. She hadn't expected to see them, and she definitely wasn't in the right head space to deal with them at the moment.
But she could play a part; she'd mastered that skill over the years.
"You're all here! Love it." Cece grabbed her now-full cup off the
counter, too busy trying to keep up appearances to notice the spores
inside the cup that were beginning to fuse together, collecting into a
pulsating, sticky black glob.

"I thought I wouldn't see you before I left for Iowa," Iris said
as Cece joined them at their table. "Literally, where have you been?"

"In Brooklyn," Cece said. She raised an eyebrow. "Remember? The place from rap songs."

"Your debate camp is just around the corner, isn't it?" Aisha asked. "How's it going?"

Cece slipped on her mask of perfection, flipped her hair, and lied, "Amazing. I'm ranked number one, obviously. But I literally see no one ever, it is so much work."

Harper rolled her eyes. "You think *you* have so much work? This internship is *insane*. I had to pull two all-nighters in a row."

Aisha nodded. "I had to pull *three* all-nighters in a row. I literally started to hallucinate. The computer science lab over at Columbia is intense and smelly. It's, like, me and a bunch of twenty-five-year-old future Mark Zuckerbergs."

Cece felt herself beginning to get short of breath as she listened to her friends talking about their uber-successful summer jobs. She had nothing and they had *everything*. She had to nail this interview to prove she was worth something; she just had to.

Iris cut in, "You think *you're* stressed out? I have to turn in my memoir by next weekend."

"Memoir?" Cece asked, her panic escalating.

"Yeah," Iris said with a shrug. "It will hopefully be coming out next spring."

"You're publishing a memoir? Now?" Cece squeaked.

Iris smiled. "I guess I've just lived more than most people my age."

Cece could feel her mask slipping. She had to get out of there before she had a full-on panic attack. "I should really take off," she said quickly. "I've got a college interview."

Her three best friends leaned in, intrigued. "Oh, with who?"

"Kathryn Bosco," Cece said. As soon as she dropped the name, she felt her faux-confidence rebuilding.

"Wow," Iris said, eyes wide. "That *is* a big appointment. She's major. Like, *the* alumni interviewer for Brown."

Aisha nodded. "She can write your ticket. You're basically already in. I know three girls she met with last year, all accepted."

Harper tossed out an obviously fake smile. "Well done, Cece. Well done."

Cece relaxed, finally feeling like she was back in control. She waved to her friends, grabbed her kombucha cup off the table, and called out, "See you guys later!" Then she slurped up a big sip, making a sour face as she swallowed a blob of something lodged in her straw: a mass of living, growing spores that had made their way from Trey's haunted car to the very bottom of her cup.

The lobby of Kathryn Bosco's law office building was upscale and intimidating. Cece took a deep breath, then stepped toward the elevators, focusing on the calming voice inside her earbuds telling her, "Inhale peace and exhale worry."

Cece repeated the instructions, muttering aloud, "I can and I will. I embrace this challenge. I embrace this—" Her voice cut out as a large burp exploded out of her from somewhere deep within. Cece looked around the lobby to see if anyone had heard it, then rubbed her stomach and boarded the elevator. *It was probably just nerves.*

Outside Kathryn's office, Cece gathered her composure and put on a mask of confidence. She stepped into the office and smiled broadly at the woman sitting behind her elegant desk. Kathryn Bosco was everything Cece wanted to be in life, and she knew her entire future was riding on this interview.

"Water?" Kathryn asked as Cece settled into the seat across from her. "Cold or room temp?"

"Oh!" Cece said, laughing nervously. "How fancy. I'll, uh, have what you're having."

Kathryn smiled at her, obviously sensing Cece's nerves. "Relax," she told her gently. "It's just an interview that will determine the rest of your life."

Cece laughed along with her, then said, "Sure, yeah. Uh, room temp. Sorry, I'm just nervous."

"Of course you're nervous," Kathryn said as her assistant handed Cece a cold water. "You're a type A girl. It's kind of in our blood. Takes one to know one." She leaned across her desk and asked, "Which one are you? The swimmer? Swimming is an intense sport."

"Um, no," Cece said, suddenly even more nervous. Did Kathryn not even know who she was? This was worse than she could have imagined. "I'm Cece Brewer. St. Agnes. I'm a girl . . . who, uh, doesn't swim. My mom's Tori Brewer."

"Tori!" Kathryn exclaimed. "Love her."

"Yeah, she's great," Cece stammered. "She's . . . my mother. So, yeah."

"You're the debater? I was a debater."

"More like *the* debater." Cece cleared her throat. "They're still talking about your final round of the Harvard National High School Forensics Tournament."

"So . . ." Kathryn said abruptly. "What's your story? You've got"—she checked her watch—"seven minutes. Kidding." Then she swiped to her calendar and cringed. "Okay, I'm not kidding. I do have a meeting in seven minutes."

Cece launched right into the speech she'd been preparing for weeks. "I recently completed my junior year at St. Agnes, where I have a 4.46 GPA and placed on the distinguished Headmaster's List. I was just named an AP Scholar with Distinction, and as you mentioned, I'm a nationally ranked debater."

"Your mom said you're doing the program at NYU. I've judged there before."

Cece opened her mouth, but rather than responding, a massive burp exploded out of her. She covered her mouth, horrified. "I'm so, so sorry. That's completely unlike me." Kathryn shifted uncomfortably in her chair, and Cece thundered on. "Anyway, I want to continue with my love for learning at Brow—" Another burp lurched out, cutting her off again. This one smelled awful, and Kathryn waved her hand in front of her nose as Cece barreled on, "This has honestly never happened to me before. Maybe I just need some water."

She reached for the glass of water and downed it. As soon as she'd finished swallowing the last of it, her nose began to bleed. "Oh!" Kathryn exclaimed, pointing. "Uh, your nose is bleeding." She passed her a tissue.

Cece dabbed at her nose, then looked at it—confused when she noticed it was not blood but rather some kind of inky black goo coming from her nose. Just then, her other nostril began to leak goo.

"Just tilt your head back," Kathryn instructed her. "I'm going to go get some more tissues."

As soon as Kathryn had left the office, Cece looked at her reflection in the office window. She watched, horrified, as the black goo coming out of her nose began to wriggle—then flow back up into her nose. "Oh no. No, it's in my mind. It's gotta be in my mind . . ." She heard a low hum, then glanced down at the tissue. It was completely clear, as if the goo had never been there at all.

Panicked, Cece jumped out of her seat and raced from the office. The hum was still ringing in her ears. She was clearly not in her right mind; something was going on, and she had to get somewhere she could think. Desperate, she staggered down the street, racing toward her mother's apartment.

As she rushed down the hall of her building, she bumped into their neighbor Bob, who called out, "I thought you were away all summer?"

Cece rushed past him, hastily unlocking the door to her apartment and slamming it shut behind her. She plowed through the bathroom door and immediately coughed up a glob of black goo in the sink. Seconds later, the hum stopped. She looked around confused, suddenly unsure how or why she was where she was. Then she glanced down at the blob of horrifying goo in the sink and muttered, "No more kombucha for me."

She quickly brushed her teeth while working to wash the blob of goo down the drain. She wiped her face on a towel, then headed for the door.

As soon as Cece stepped into the quiet of the hallway, the glob of goo bubbled back up and out of the bathroom drain . . .

CHAPTER EIGHTEEN

"Hey," Alex said, coming up behind Frankie and Devin in the hospital waiting area. "How's Trey doing?"

"Still not talking," Frankie answered.

"Just staring," Devin added. As Alex pushed some buttons on the vending machine, Devin's phone rang. It was his sister. "Hey, Cece," he said, answering quickly.

"I'm at the apartment," Cece told him. "But I don't know how I got here."

"What do you mean?"

"I was at that college interview nearby and then all of a sudden I came to, and I was here."

"You don't remember how you got there?" Devin asked, growing more and more worried.

"No."

"Cece, slow down. This is important. Did you hear a hum?"

Cece nodded, even though her brother couldn't see her through the phone. "Oh my god. Devin, I think whatever happened to you happened to me."

"I'll be right there," Devin promised. He hung up and turned to his friends. "Cece's in trouble. I have to go."

"I'm coming with you," Frankie insisted.

"I'm coming, too," Alex said.

The three friends left the hospital and raced toward the subway, unsure what they'd find when they made it uptown.

Back at the apartment, while Cece waited for her brother to arrive, she decided to deal with her kombucha cup. She held it over the kitchen sink and poured the remaining contents down the drain. "You have gone baaaaad," she said as she turned on the garbage disposal. Cece stifled a burp; whatever was in that kombucha was seriously messed up.

As she turned back around, Cece knocked over a container of cooking utensils, and it shattered as it hit the floor. "Oh, great." She bent down to pick up the shards and a whisk that had rolled halfway across the kitchen. As she righted herself, Cece gasped. For there, directly in front of her, was a large, quivering black mass of *something*. "What in the mother are you?" she gasped.

She took a step to the left, then the right, but the Monster Blood tracked her every move. Cece took a tentative step forward, hoping to step past it to flee back to the kitchen . . . but the gelatinous mass of goo began to envelop her foot. She pushed at it, desperately trying to free herself, but then her hand began to sink in, too. "No!" Cece screamed, terrified.

The Monster Blood began to gurgle as it pulled her in, trying to absorb her completely. "Let go of me!" Cece squealed. Desperate, she pressed her other leg and arm against the doorframe. With a burst of adrenaline, she was finally able to extricate herself from the blobby grasp and tumbled into the living room. As Cece scrambled back to her feet, her breath caught in her throat when she saw that the Monster Blood was now looming in front of her, blocking the exit.

She scanned the room, searching for any kind of weapon. Cece swept a fire poker into her hand and hit the Monster Blood with it—but the metal just lodged into the gooey mess and got stuck in the blob. As it absorbed the weapon, the mass began creeping toward Cece, devouring chairs and tables as it slithered across the room, hungry. It consumed Cece's bag and then the entire couch. It kept advancing, unstoppable.

Cece backed away, then spun and ran toward her bedroom, slamming the door behind her. She wedged a chair in the door to keep it closed, then hustled toward the window. Panicked, she pulled on the window, but it wouldn't budge. Her eyes quickly darted to the door, which was bulging under the weight of the Monster Blood pushing from the other side.

Suddenly, everything went silent.

Cece froze, knowing—in this case—that quiet wasn't good. Seconds later, the Monster Blood began *pouring* under the door, covering most of the floor in a mere instant. Cece scrambled up onto her bed, trying to avoid the spill. Then she spotted her bookshelf. If she could knock it over, maybe she could create a sort of bridge to cross the room and escape. She threw the shelf to the ground, watching as all her medals, trophies, books, and certificates were absorbed by the pool of ooze. Every trace of her glory was devoured, digested by the Monster Blood.

Without a look back, Cece bounded over the shelf bridge, leaped onto her rolling desk chair, and rode it from the room and out into the hall. As she moved toward the front door of the apartment, she pushed everything she could find into the Monster Blood's path, trying to slow it down as it surged after her. Then just when Cece thought the path was clear, she reached the front door and skidded to a stop. Somehow, the Monster Blood had split, and a portion of the blob was still blocking the exit.

As she came to a sudden, horrified stop, she knocked into a lamp. The whole thing crashed to the floor, the bulb breaking and sparking on the floor behind her. The Monster Blood flowed over it, moving steadily toward her—and then suddenly stopped. The electricity coursing from the bulb hardened it, and Cece watched, fascinated, as she discovered the beast's weakness.

The goo encircled her, trapping her in the center of the pool as it closed in, growing closer by the moment. Cece knew her only hope was to get to the lamp and somehow try to use the electricity to hold it back. But her circle of safety was rapidly shrinking, and she couldn't reach it. The Monster Blood rose up, poised to strike. Cece was frozen with fear as the pool of goo began to release a dense cloud of spores that swirled around her. She began to hear the now familiar hum, her eyes began to ooze black, then everything went still.

"Cece!" Suddenly, the front door flew open as Devin screamed her name. Alex and Frankie rushed in behind him, and Cece startled out of whatever trance she'd been trapped under. She blinked away the black tears, and the Monster Blood changed course, flowing now toward the door and the three new arrivals.

"What the—?" Alex said, her eyes wide. Before she could finish her question, the Monster Blood lunged at them. But before it could strike, Cece grabbed her stun gun and slammed it into the pool of goo. The top of the creature began to harden and crystallize, hit with the sudden jolt of electricity.

"What is happening?" Frankie gasped.

"I was about to ask you!" Cece replied. One of the remaining sections of Monster Blood snapped at her, but she dodged it and then zapped it with the gun. "We have to destroy this thing!"

"Obviously!" Alex said. "How?"

Cece suddenly spotted her kombucha cup across the room. "Help me get it to the kitchen!" she cried, spinning around. As they wrestled with the blob, trying to usher it into the kitchen, Cece turned on the garbage disposal and they all worked together to try to stuff pieces of it down into the drain. The last bit of goo tried to flee, but Cece was able to zap it with the stun gun and stuff it down the drain, too. Finally, exhausted, she dropped her weapon and collapsed to the ground.

While the group waited for the subway that would take them back out to Gravesend, they finally had a chance to talk about what had happened.

"She had black tears like you did," Frankie said, gesturing to Devin. "At the fort."

"And you couldn't remember anything, either," Cece reminded her brother.

Devin nodded. "I just don't understand what Dad said about it all connecting to Uncle Matty."

Cece took in a deep breath, then tried to let the events of the day go with a big sigh. She began to cry as the weight of everything hit. "Thank you, guys, so much for coming to help me. Even though I didn't deserve it. I've been such a raging jerk. Not listening to any of you. Alex, you tried to tell me."

"More than once," Alex said with a smirk.

"Devin, I'm just . . ." Cece began. "I'm so sorry. I act like I'm so much more put together. But I'm a total mess. I was at the apartment because I haven't been going to debate camp."

Devin's mouth hung open. "What? Why?"

"Because . . . because I didn't get in."

"They didn't take you?" he asked. "But you're so great at debate."

"You're only 'great' until you're in a room full of greats. When everyone is great, if you aren't the best, you're nobody. I'm smart, but I'm not the smartest. I'm pretty, but not the prettiest. I'm a good debater, but I wasn't the best. I wasn't even close. I'm a fraud. I don't even know who I am anymore."

Alex lifted her chin and said, "I think you're a pretty rad girl. From my perspective."

Cece offered her a weak smile in return.

"Why didn't you tell me?" Devin asked.

"Because I didn't want to see that look you have on your face right now. Pity."

Devin shook his head. "I'm not looking at you with pity, Cece. I'm finally looking at you as human. For once it actually feels like

138

we're really twins. You're a mess! Like me! Like a real, honest, lying mess! This is fantastic! I've never felt closer to you."

They hugged, then Cece smiled. "Let's go home."

The subway car pulled into the station and the group boarded. As Devin, Frankie, and Cece sat, Alex leaned against the doors of the car. "So wait," she said to Cece, trying to get all the facts of the day straight. "You're telling me you coughed that thing up?"

"I brushed my teeth after," Cece said with a cringe. "What the hell was that stuff, though? It just covered *everything*. Ew. Drippy. Black. Goo. So disgusting . . ."

Just then, the train lurched to a stop in the middle of a pitch-black tunnel. "We're being held here momentarily," the conductor's voice said over the speakers. "The train will be moving shortly." The electricity blinked on and off, and several passengers groaned at the delay.

That's when Cece noticed something trickling down the subway windows behind Alex, who was still leaning against the doors. It was black, drippy, disgusting goo. Her eyes went wide as the lights in the train blinked off and realization hit: The Monster Blood was back.

CHAPTER NINETEEN

"It's here," Cece whispered to the others. She pointed to the windows of the train, which were covered in black liquid goo. "What do we do?" Devin asked.

"We gotta go!" Alex said, grabbing Cece's arm to pull her toward the door that led to the next train car. Each time they passed from one car to the next, they could see the massive silhouette of the Monster Blood following them, oozing across the top of the stalled-out train. When they got to the last car, they saw that the mass of goo had beat them there. A little droplet wriggled its way through a cracked window and splatted onto the floor as Alex looked around helplessly. "There's nowhere else to go!"

Cece took a deep breath, then told the others, "It's been following me all day, like it's attracted to me or something. I have to take care of it myself." She glanced at her brother, who looked nervous, then turned to Alex—and impulsively kissed her. Then before any of them could react, Cece opened the door at the end of the car and jumped onto the tracks below.

She raced through the tunnel, the Monster Blood in close pursuit. Up ahead, she could see her target—the electrified third rail of the subway system. As Cece leaped over the rail, the Monster Blood lunged after her . . . and was shocked into stillness by the third rail's electricity.

An oncoming train blasted its horn. Then moments later, the subway car collided with the crystallized glob of goo, smashing it into a thousand spores. Cece dragged herself to the nearest subway station, breathless. "Cece!" Devin said as the others rushed toward her. He grabbed her arm and hefted her up onto the platform beside him. "I know you said not to say this, but . . . that was bussin'!"

Cece shook her head and told him, "We better figure out what the hell is going on. Like, now."

Not long afterward, a car service dropped the group at the entrance to Fort Jerome—the place where this had started all those years ago with Uncle Matty and his friends.

As they got out of the car, Frankie leaned over and gave Devin a quick kiss and he kissed her back. She'd begun to understand you couldn't go through something like this with someone and *not* realize that each moment was precious, that anything could happen. No one else noticed the kiss, but both Frankie and Devin knew something had changed between them.

"Hey," Alex said as they all headed toward the tunnel system. "Is that your dad's car?"

Cece glanced over; Anthony's Volvo was there, suggesting their dad had also returned to the tunnels to scope some things out. They walked on, diving into the fort's dark tunnel system.

At that moment, deep inside the tunnel, Anthony was desperately trying to fix what he'd inadvertently started. He held up

Matty's sweatshirt inside the old control room and muttered, "I don't know what's going on, but I know I have to let this go. I have to let *you* go and try to stop whatever it is happening because of it."

He put the hoodie on the floor and took out a matchbook. As he struck the match and leaned down to touch the flame to the sweatshirt, the hoodie slid across the floor and settled atop the hatch in the floor. Anthony walked toward it, investigating.

Just as the four teens got to the edge of the control room and spotted Anthony inside, standing over the sweatshirt, a hum started up from the space below.

Devin had heard this sound before; he knew exactly what it meant. He spun around to the other three teens and screamed, "Ruuuuunnn!"

Anthony was so focused on the control room and the mysteriously moving sweatshirt that he hadn't even noticed he wasn't alone in the tunnels. Inside his hazmat suit, Anthony felt safe and protected from whatever might emerge from the depths of the tunnels, and so he forged forward, eager to continue with his investigation. He dragged himself back to the fading memories of the night he'd last seen his brother, and tried to use them to guide him now.

As the hum from beneath the floor grew louder, Anthony moved toward the electrical panel on the other side of the room, reaching his hand out to touch it. "This started it," he muttered to himself.

Anthony opened his toolbox and pried the panel open, surprised to see that the electronics inside the panel were glowing. "It has power?"

Curious, he reached his arm inside the electrical console, feeling around until he hit a wire with his gloved hand. He traced along the wire to a button and pressed it—little blue sparks shooting out of the panel at his action. With a whoosh, the hatch on the floor slid open. Anthony stepped toward the open hole and peered down into the dusty abyss. His flashlight caught the edge of a metal ladder that led down to a catwalk below. "An underground chamber . . ." Anthony mused. "What is this place?"

As he stood there, a rush of spores emerged from the hole, like bats exploding out of a cave. They swarmed Anthony, but his protective suit kept him safe from the spores. Even more confused, Anthony scrambled back to the console and quickly reached inside to press the switch again. The hatch sealed shut, and Anthony scurried out of the tunnel.

At his car, with his kids and their friends secretly and quietly watching from nearby, he pulled out the personal decontamination unit he'd brought along—just in case. And as he'd suspected, he needed it! He entered the unit, and seconds later, steam and vapors from the cleansing chemicals hit. As soon as it was safe, he pulled off his helmet and gloves and began to record a voice memo, eager to capture his discovery. "I have discovered an underground chamber beneath the tunnel's control room," he said into his phone. "I believe that my brother, Matty Brewer, did not drown but possibly went down there. The chamber is the source of the dangerous organic matter. I need more equipment before I can safely explore it."

Removing the remainder of the protective gear from his body, Anthony felt satisfied that he'd done what he could for now. Unfortunately, Anthony didn't notice the tiny tear on the wrist of his suit, which had left him wholly vulnerable to the terrifying spores inside the tunnel . . .

CHAPTER TWENTY

C J was not a great delivery person; even *he* could see that. But it was only because he was always being asked to work below his ability, untested in the areas where he knew he would *truly* shine.

His mom was giving him one of her lectures after another case of "disappearing deliveries," but this time she seemed entirely serious. "We can't just give out free food and refunds because you didn't deliver the orders. This business is barely breaking even," she told him. "I don't want to switch to contracting with DoorDash, but I will if I have to."

"I have a solution for that," CJ told her, exuding charm. "I take over as manager."

"You can't even make deliveries," his mom, Gwen, reminded him.

"I should be upper management, Mom. I have ideas. First, we gotta rebrand. 'Gwendolyn's' is moldy. This place . . . is G-Dubs. Or Gwendy's. Or Gwen's Organic."

"We don't serve anything organic," Gwen reminded him.

"FDA has no hard-and-fast rules as to what's organic. And it sounds good."

"It does sound good."

CJ was all fired up and went on, "We give the option to burrito-fy or smoothie-fy any entrée on the menu. Add acai bowls. Cut the ten worst-selling items to save cash. I'm looking at you, liver and onions."

"That does make sense."

"Take a chance on me," CJ finished. "And I will bring your amazing cooking to the next generation of Gravesendelinos."

"You're really serious about this?"

"Dead serious," CJ said seriously. "You and me are going to be the next Five Guys."

Gwen smiled. "I like seeing this side of you. Okay, if you show me you can be real with me, I'll talk to your father about it."

Frankie, Devin, and Cece had had a restless night. After everything that had happened the day before, and the questions about how exactly their dad was involved in what was happening, the twins decided to spend the night at Frankie's instead of home. "Hey," Frankie said, startling Cece and Devin awake. "I gotta go to work."

"Work?" Devin asked, scrambling to sitting. "At a time like this?"

"What else are we supposed to do?" Frankie asked.

The three of them glanced out the window to where Anthony's car was parked in front of his house. "He's still in there," Devin noted.

"Should we go to the police?" Cece asked tentatively.

"And say what?" Devin asked her. "You barfed a kombucha monster into existence because our dad's a mad scientist? We don't know anything yet."

"Well," Frankie said, heading for the door. "I know I have to go to work and my mom is going to be home soon."

Hearing that, the twins decided to join Frankie at work. As soon as they got to the coffee shop, Frankie gestured around the small space and said, "Make yourselves useful." She tossed Devin a towel and he sighed.

While they worked on opening up, Cece suddenly gasped and blurted out, "You guys, I just realized—when you crushed that Trey-monster with the Oldsmobile . . . I was *in* the car with Alex the very next day. And Alex kept saying the car was alive."

Devin tossed the towel aside and said, "We need to find Alex!"

They all rushed for the exit, but stopped when the door burst open and Joe Junior entered. He gave Frankie a big hug, then said, "Look at her. The world's best future daughter-in-law."

Frankie and Devin exchanged a guilty look. She grinned sheepishly at Joe Junior and said, "Oh, I don't know about that . . ."

"Well, guess who's finally awake to thank you himself?" Joe Junior said happily. "Trey."

"So," Devin said, "is he talking?"

"Yep! And he's asking for Frankie."

Devin put on a fake smile and blurted out, "Splendid!"

Joe Junior gave him a weird look, then went on, "The doctors say he's going to be released this afternoon. He wants you to be there when he gets home."

"Of course," Frankie promised. "I'll be there. How great."

Devin nodded. "That really is such *splendid* news." Noticing the looks the others were giving him, he shrugged and said, "Cece told me I couldn't' say bussin' anymore."

Cece rolled her eyes. "Well, that's not any better."

As Jen drove Alex to community service that morning, she decided it was as good a time as any to ask her a few questions. "Alex, look," she began. "Anthony told me something at the hospital." Alex grabbed her bag and orange vest, then glanced at her mom questioningly. "He said something may have attacked Devin. And possibly Trey."

Alex turned and studied her mom. Was she being real?

Jen continued, "Did someone attack you? When you were in Trey's car?"

"Not someone. *Something*. But you're not going to believe me."

"Try me," Jen said.

"His car. It was alive. It drove itself. And not in, like, a Tesla way. It sounds crazy, but I know I'm not crazy."

"Alex, listen to me closely. You're in danger."

"What does that mean? What are you not telling me?" Alex glared at her mom, wishing they could just be honest with each other.

"You're just going to have to trust me," Jen told her. "Do not get involved. I'm going to handle this for both of us."

Alex studied her mom, realizing again—for the first time in a very long time—that her mom obviously had her back. She nodded. "Okay."

CHAPTER TWENTY-ONE

Anthony checked the time as he staggered into the kitchen the morning after his adventure in the Fort Jerome tunnels, and saw that he'd slept until eleven—which was very unlike him. Despite the extra sleep, he felt like crap. He was freezing but hot at the same time, and he sneezed as he walked through the room. Shuffling toward the cupboard, he reached for a bottle of pills and swallowed one down, then grabbed the thermometer and took his temperature. "Eighty-six degrees?" he asked, shaking the thermometer. "That can't be right. How old is this thing?"

He grabbed a Gwendolyn's menu off the fridge door and dialed the number. "Hey, Gwen," he said when she picked up. "It's Anthony. Can you send CJ over with a big bowl of chicken soup? I've got a summer cold." Then he sneezed again and tossed the tissue in the trash—not noticing that the mucus that had come out of his nose was a thick, black goo.

Not long afterward, there was a knock and Anthony threw open the front door to find CJ holding a delivery bag. CJ jumped backward when he saw how ragged Anthony looked, but he tried to play it off. "Hey, Plant Man! Lookin' good, boss."

"Good?" Anthony said, his voice scratchy. "I don't look like I'm about to keel over?"

"Would I lie to you? That'll be nineteen dollars. I factored in a twenty-five percent gratuity, but feel free to go over."

Anthony patted his pockets, finding them empty. "Aw, crap. Come inside, let me find my wallet." Just as he reached for his bag on a nearby chair, he was surprised by another fit of sneezing. He turned back toward CJ, even as he continued to sneeze into his hands.

"Wow," CJ mused. "You're really in bad shape."

Anthony stopped sneezing and stared down into his hands.

"Everything okay?" CJ asked slowly, noticing Anthony remained hunched over. He began to back away, not wanting to catch whatever it was this guy was dealing with. "Hey, man, don't worry about the money. I'll let my mom know." Anthony continued to sway, still not standing upright. "Mr. Brewer, are you okay?"

Anthony finally stood up straight. CJ gasped; Anthony's eyeball was dangling out of his eye, hanging by a nerve, and it was dripping in black goo.

As CJ spun to flee, Anthony screamed after him, "LEAVE!"

CJ raced to the restaurant, totally horrified by what he'd just seen. His mom caught him as he fled into the back, demanding, "CJ, why aren't you delivering the food? I'm getting complaints from everyone this morning!"

"I can explain," CJ said quickly. "Mr. Brewer. He—well, his eye—" He suddenly realized how crazy this was going to sound, but he had to tell *someone*. "Mr. Brewer's eyeball *fell out*. It was just, like, dangling from his head."

Gwen stared at him in disbelief. "What?"

"And it was covered in this black stuff. I'm serious. It was scary!"

"Black stuff?"

"I'm not lying," CJ promised.

His mom seemed to believe him. She took off her apron and said, "Okay, then. Mike, you're in charge. Hold the delivery orders."

"Where are you going?" CJ asked.

"To check on Anthony. If you're telling the truth, he probably needs help."

"It was scary, Mom," CJ said, shaking his head. "I don't think we should go back there."

"CJ, just save us both the trip," Gwen sighed, obviously frustrated. "Is this one of your stories again?"

CJ shook his head. "No."

She pushed through the back door and stepped out to the street. "I'll drive." She popped on the scooter and gestured for CJ to get on behind her.

When they got to Anthony's house, CJ dragged his feet. "Look, I don't think we should be here. I can just cover the missing deliveries out of my paycheck."

Gwen ignored him and knocked on the door. "Anthony? It's Gwen. You okay?"

The front door swung open, and Anthony stepped outside. CJ studied him. Just minutes ago, he'd looked like he was on death's door . . . but now he looked *normal*. "Oh, hey, Gwen!" Anthony said cheerfully.

"Mom, I swear," CJ said quickly. "His eyeball was in his hand."

Anthony laughed. "Uh, I'm fine. Thank you. CJ, you are hilarious. Oh—" He grabbed his wallet from his pocket and held out a few bills. "Sorry I didn't have cash earlier. Here you go. For the soup. And, CJ, for your troubles." He handed CJ a twenty, along with a look that said *Drop it*. Anthony chuckled again and smiled at Gwen. "Who knows how kids get these ideas. Too many horror shows on TV, I say. Gotta be careful what they stream into their little brains. Screenagers, am I right?"

"You're so right, Anthony," Gwen agreed. "Feel better."

Anthony turned and went back inside his house as Gwen began to leave. CJ looked from the front door to his mom, imploring again, "Mom, I'm telling you—"

"Enough," Gwen snapped. "No more lies. I thought you were ready to really help this family. But it turns out that was a lie, too. You can forget about being a manager. You can forget about being a delivery driver."

"Are you firing me? I'm your son!"

"And you always will be. But you're no longer my employee. Keys." Gwen held out her hand and CJ reluctantly dropped the keys to the scooter into her open palm. "Phone," she said next. "It's a business account." CJ reluctantly handed her his phone, too. Then she popped on the front of the scooter and motioned for CJ to slide in behind her. "Get on."

As they zoomed away, his mom driving his beloved scooter, CJ glanced back at the Brewer house. *Something* was up with Anthony, that much he knew for sure.

Inside his house, Anthony watched CJ and Gwen zip off. That was close. Too close.

He hustled down to his basement workroom and glanced in the mirror. He put his fingers up to his eye, grabbed it, and tugged it out again. "Why is this happening?" he asked his own reflection.

Suddenly, something dawned on him. He rushed over to the hazmat suit he'd worn inside the tunnels the previous night. He scoured every inch of it, hoping his suspicions weren't true. But then, right by the area where his glove met his arm, there was a tiny tear in the protective fabric of the suit. He closed his eyes and sighed. "This is not good."

When he got back to the restaurant, CJ tried to process everything that had happened. "I see a guy with an eyeball hanging from his face and I freak out and she *fires* me? Her own son?" he muttered. "Who does that? And why won't she believe me? I've never lied to her. And if I ever did lie, it was probably to reveal a deeper truth." Just then, the restaurant phone rang. Out of habit, CJ reached for it and answered, "Gwen's, this is CJ." Then he remembered what had just happened and said, "I no longer work here."

On the other end of the line, Anthony's voice said, "CJ, it's Anthony. I owe you an explanation."

"Um, yeah, you do."

"Look," Anthony said with a deep sigh. "I need you to come back."

"I'm not going back there."

"It's not what you think, CJ."

"That's good, because I think your eyeball was dangling out of your head."

"I can explain everything. And I'll explain it to your mom, too. I'll get you your job back if you just come back over here and help me with something. Please. It will all make sense soon."

"If I show up," CJ said slowly, "are you going to murder me?"

"No."

"Do you promise?"

"Yes. Although I should point out that if I was capable of murder, I wouldn't have any problem breaking a promise."

"Ha," CJ said, finally smiling. "Okay, Mr. Brewer. You sound like yourself. I'll be right there."

When he walked up to the house soon after, Anthony answered the door immediately and then gave him a curious look. "Okay," CJ said. "I'm ready for an explanation."

"What are you talking about?"

"What are *you* talking about?" CJ repeated with a laugh. "You told me to come over here. That you were going to tell me every-thing and fix stuff with my mom."

"I did?"

"Yeah, boss. You did. So spill it."

Suddenly, a look of fear crossed Anthony's face. Then he screamed out, "RUN!"

CJ jumped, then spun to flee. What the heck was happening? But before he could take two steps, Anthony grabbed the hood of CJ's sweatshirt, dragged him into the house, and slammed the door shut with his foot.

CHAPTER TWENTY-TWO

D evin, Cece, and Frankie entered the park, hunting for Alex. "She said she's by the playground," Cece said, pointing. "Over there!"

"What do you guys want?" Alex asked as her friends approached.

"I'm sorry I didn't believe you about the car," Cece said quickly.

"What car?" Alex asked, all defenses up after her mom's warning that morning.

"Trey's car," Cece answered. "You said it was alive and you weren't in control. And I didn't believe you, which wasn't cool of me. It's time for me to start trusting you. For us to start trusting—"

Alex cut her off. "I was just messing with you, girl. Can't believe you fell for it."

Frankie gave her a confused look. "That wasn't what you were saying at the hospital."

"What are you guys talking about?" Alex asked.

Cece shook her head. "Alex, why are you doing this?"

Alex shrugged. "Whatever it is you guys are up to, I don't want to be a part of it. I'm already in trouble. I don't want to get into more." She stood up and tossed her lunch into a nearby garbage can, then returned to her community service group.

"I'll try to talk to her," Cece told the others.

She quickly caught up with Alex, who spun around and said, "What did you not understand about 'I don't want to be a part of this?'"

"Is this about how I shut you down?" Cece asked. "After the crash? It's just, the car thing really scared me. It's not that I'm not into you, but I did not know what to do with that."

Alex scoffed. "I told you the truth, and you didn't believe me. You don't get to come back from that."

Cece nodded. "Okay, that's fair. But where does this leave us?"

Alex shook her head sadly. "There is no 'us.'" Then she walked away again, filled with regret, disappointment, and questions about what might have been.

After Cece had gone after Alex, Devin glanced at Frankie and said, "So, I guess it's just you and me . . ." He reached for her hand, but she pulled it away quickly.

"I should head over to Trey's."

"Seriously?" Devin scoffed.

"Yes. Seriously."

"You broke up with him. Remember?"

"Devin, Trey has been in the hospital. In a coma."

"Catatonic state, technically. I Googled it. And it was pretty brief. I mean, these things can go on for months—"

Frankie sighed. "The point is he's been there for me when I needed him. And now he needs me. I'm sorry."

"That's a cop-out."

Frankie glared at him. "That sounds like what somebody who's never been needed would say." She turned and walked away, leaving Devin alone.

"I'm needed," he told no one. "I'm super needed." Frustrated, he wandered down a path near the water.

He began to hear a slight hum, but he was distracted from the sound when he heard a girl's voice call out, "Hey!"

Devin spun around, spotting a girl around his age sitting on a park bench. "Hey, do I know you?"

"I don't know," the girl said with a flirty smile. "Do you?" She patted the empty seat next to her. "That's the universal gesture for 'Take a seat.'" Devin shook his head, as if to clear it. For some reason, he was immediately drawn to the girl. There was something magnetic about her, something that was pulling him in. He glanced at her again, noticing that she was listening to music on an old Discman from the nineties. "I'm Hannah," she told him, pulling off her headphones.

"I'm Devin," he said, realizing he was already totally smitten.

"What's wrong?" Hannah asked him.

"Nothing's wrong," Devin said quickly, not wanting to offload his problems with Frankie onto this new, gorgeous girl he'd just met. "Why? Does it seem like something's wrong?"

"Well, now it does," she said, her smile lighting up her whole face.

"This girl . . ." Devin said, suddenly unable to control his own words. "This girl who I've liked for a long time . . . well, I'm starting to think it's never going to happen."

"That doesn't make any sense."

"Why not?"

Hannah grinned at him. "'Cause you're cute."

"*I'm* cute?" Devin said with a laugh. "No girl has ever called me cute."

"Well, alert the press, 'cause today one did." Hannah smiled at him, and Devin was totally captivated by her. Bewitched, even.

"You're like a breath of fresh air," Devin said after they'd talked for a while longer. This was going great; where had *this* girl been all his life? "You're, like, the first good thing that's happened to me all summer. I couldn't even begin to explain it all to you—"

"Because you were at the fort," Hannah said seriously.

Devin blinked. "How do you know I was at the fort?"

"I've been to the fort, too," Hannah said seriously. "They call it Camp Nightmare."

"Why?"

"A lot of bad stuff happened out there," Hannah told him. "A long time ago."

"How do you know?" Devin asked.

"I'll show you." Hannah stood up, and the hum Devin had been hearing the whole time they'd been talking began to intensify. But now the hum was comforting. Enchanting.

"Okay . . ." Devin said and stood up to follow her.

"I'm so sorry," Anthony said as he hastily tied CJ to a chair in the basement using luggage bungees. "I'm so, so sorry."

CJ pleaded with him, all the while knowing it was useless. "Please just let me go."

"I can't."

"Why are you doing this?" CJ begged.

"No one can know of our existence until it's time."

"What?" CJ blurted.

Anthony looked totally confused. "Why did I just say that?"

"I don't know!" CJ shrieked. "I don't know why you're doing anything you're doing. Why are you asking me?"

"I can't let you out of here," Anthony told him firmly. "Not yet."

"Well, when, man?"

"Soon," Anthony promised. "I just need to give you something first." He moved toward his work desk, grabbing a beaker off a shelf. CJ watched as Anthony spat a tiny bit of black goo into the beaker. Then he stirred it around, as if he were preparing a cup of tea. "Drink this," he ordered.

"Um, no thank you."

"I'm sorry, CJ," Anthony said, sounding pained. "I don't want to do this."

"Then don't! Please, Mr. Brewer!"

"You're right," Anthony said, obviously struggling with

something internally. "What am I doing? This is wrong." He backed up, and his body convulsed with conflicting plans. "I should let you go." He moved toward CJ, then stopped again. "But I can't. I have to do this. It's for the greater good."

"Oh, c'mon," CJ moaned.

Anthony leaned toward him, the beaker of dark liquid held at the ready. But just as Anthony went to pour it into CJ's mouth, CJ slammed his forehead forward. *Crack!* It wasn't the glass, but Anthony's *finger* that had cracked on impact.

CJ was totally grossed out by the sight of Anthony's finger, bent and twisted backward. But Anthony was clearly fascinated. "Huh. Well, would you look at that?" He took it in his other hand, twisting the finger back into place with a sickening crunch.

Moments later, the doorbell rang. Anthony hastily tied a bandanna around CJ's mouth, muttered, "Not a word . . . ," then headed up the stairs. Opening the door, he was surprised to find Jen standing on the other side. "Jen. Hey."

"Are you feeling okay?" Jen asked, studying him closely.

"I'm great!" Anthony lied. "Doing great. Everything's great."

Jen pushed past him into the house. "Hey, I'm sorry to bother you—"

Anthony could hear distant sounds of CJ struggling to free himself from the bandanna and ties in the basement. He knew he had to get Jen out of the house before the kid was successful. Because this looked *bad*. "You know," he told her quickly, "I'm a little under the weather today . . ."

"What's that?" Jen asked as the sound of muffled noises echoed up from below.

"I don't hear anything," Anthony said loudly.

"You don't have another kid in your basement, do you?" Jen said with a laugh.

Anthony tried to laugh along with her. "Oh, that. No, it's just the neighbor's TV."

Jen took a deep breath, then got to the point. "I'm here because I have something for you." She held up a package, a tin box she'd dug up in the park earlier that day. Inside was something she'd hidden thirty years ago and never thought she'd go back for again—until now.

"What's . . ." Anthony started, looking at the item in Jen's hand. "What's this?"

"I'm sorry I haven't been listening to you. I believe you now. Something happened to Alex, too. And I think you're right about Matty and the others." She opened the tin box and pulled out an old VHS tape sealed inside a plastic bag. "It's the tape from that night at the fort. I took it. And I hid it. I could never bring myself to watch it. But we need to watch it now."

He quickly snatched the box and tape out of her hand. "All these years you lied to me?" he yelled. "This wasn't yours to take. This is *Matty's*!"

"I know, I'm sorry—"

"You call yourself a cop. You're a disgrace," Anthony said, then ushered her out the door and slammed it closed behind her.

CHAPTER TWENTY-THREE

Frankie brought a smoothie out onto Trey's front porch and handed it to him. "Extra protein powder," she said with a gentle smile, welcoming him home. "Just like you like it."

"So good. Thank you," Trey said, accepting it gratefully. "I love you."

Frankie bristled slightly, then smiled again. "I know."

"It's okay," Trey assured her. "You don't have to love me back. I know I blew that. And I'm sorry that I've been such a jerk. But this whole near-death experience, it gives you perspective. I want to be different. You know, be a better Trey."

"We don't have to talk about this now—"

Trey cut her off. "Yeah. We do. I'm serious. This changed me. For so long, I've just been so insecure about myself. And so I lashed out at you. Put you down to make me feel better. And that's not cool. That's not cool at all. You had every reason to break up with me."

"You're being oddly profound right now," Frankie said, mesmerized.

"Just took me almost dying."

"So you remember?" Frankie asked him. "The breakup?"

"Of course I remember."

"Look, I'm sorry about that."

"No, it's good," Trey told her. "It's necessary. If we get back together, I want it to be because I earned it."

"I didn't think you'd remember what happened that day."

"I remember everything up until I broke into that basement. After that, it's all blank."

"What's the last thing you *do* remember?"

Trey shook his head. "I don't know. But I can't get the image of Planthony—*Anthony's*—freezer out of my head."

"What's in his freezer?"

"Not sure," Trey said, staring off at nothing. "But whatever happened to me has something to do with it." He shifted his focus to the Brewer house, across the street. "Maybe I need to go back there . . ."

"Come on, Devin. There's so much I want to show you," Hannah said over her shoulder as they walked down the path toward Fort Jerome.

"But I don't want to go back there," Devin said, even as his body was very willingly following wherever Hannah led him.

"Yes, you do."

"Right," Devin said, nodding. "I do want to go back there."

Just then, Devin's phone rang. "Don't answer that," Hannah ordered.

Devin glanced down at the screen. When he saw Frankie's

picture, he snapped out of whatever daze he'd been operating under and pressed accept. "Hey, Frankie."

"Devin," Frankie said. "Trey remembered something about the basement. Meet us at your house."

"Is that the girl?" Hannah asked. "The one who doesn't appreciate you?" Devin nodded, numb. The hum surrounding him intensified again. Hannah gestured for him to follow. "You have to come with me, Devin."

Devin considered his options for a moment, then spoke into the phone. "Sorry. I can't. I'm with Hannah."

"Who's Hannah?" Frankie asked from the other end of the line. She was already standing on Anthony's front porch and had really hoped Devin would be in for this mission.

"She's someone I met at the park."

"Devin," Frankie said firmly. "This is important. I need you."

"You need me?"

"Yes! Please! You gotta come. Right away." Frankie's words were enough to break Devin out of his spell again just long enough that he could back away.

The farther he got from Hannah, the lower the hum became. He called back to her, "I gotta go. I'm sorry. I'll come back. I promise!" And then he left to meet Frankie.

After Jen left the house, Anthony rushed back downstairs to where he'd tied up CJ. The poor kid had tried—and failed—to call for help.

Luckily, Jen hadn't heard him clearly enough. "Sorry about that, CJ," Anthony called out as he hit the bottom stair. "Nobody's saving you today. Time to drink up."

But then Anthony noticed CJ's chair was empty, toppled onto the floor. Obviously, the kid had slipped his ties and was now hidden somewhere in the basement. "CJ?" Anthony called out again, scanning the space. He couldn't have gone far; Anthony knew he had to be hiding nearby. "I know you're in here somewhere . . ."

Just as Anthony peeked behind a large piece of furniture, CJ jumped out from his hiding spot and tackled Anthony from behind, knocking him into a shelf of plants. The shelf crashed down on top of him, giving CJ time to run. He took off for the stairs, knowing he only had a couple seconds' head start. But just as he hit the middle of the staircase, Anthony grabbed him by the ankle and pulled him back down. "Sorry," Anthony said, sounding truly apologetic even as he spun CJ around and flung him into the desk. "Sorry!"

Anthony pinned CJ down against the flat surface, then pursed his lips, preparing to spit black goo directly into CJ's mouth. CJ thrashed and wriggled, but it was no use. Anthony was stronger than he was, driven by whatever passion or *creature* had possessed him, and he had the upper hand—literally. Just as CJ prepared to accept his fate, a bat swung at them from out of nowhere—and knocked Anthony's head right off his body.

Only Anthony's torso was left, hovering over CJ's still-trapped form. CJ quickly pushed the headless body away and saw Trey standing a few feet away, wielding a bat.

From the stairs, Cece began to scream.

"It's okay, Cec," Anthony's head called out from where it had rolled across the floor. "Dad's okay." Seeing the head speak, separate from Anthony's body, caused everyone else to scream as well.

"What's with all the screaming?" Devin cried, rushing down the stairs. He stepped into the basement and saw his dad's decapitated head lying on its cheek.

"Hey, Dev," the head said.

"Ahhhhh!" Devin screamed.

"Little help, please?" Anthony pleaded. As the group all continued to scream, they ran out of the basement. "Guys!" Anthony called after them. "Guys! Come back!"

Slamming the basement door shut behind them, Devin turned to the others and asked, "What the hell did you do to Dad?!"

"That wasn't Dad, right?" Cece asked, hoping what had just happened had been some sort of figment of her imagination. "Right?"

"No," Frankie said. "It couldn't have been. It was like when we killed Trey."

Trey swiveled around to look at her. "Sorry, babe, what did you do?"

Devin shrugged. "She smashed you with your car."

"What?" Trey asked.

"You weren't you. That's my point," Frankie clarified.

"I was with that thing all day," CJ told the others. "I don't know what he is, but he sure as hell isn't your dad. Although he does have some of your dad's odd mannerisms. He could be partially your dad. He did tell me a botany joke. But whatever he is, we can't let it get out."

The group began to pile furniture in front of the basement door, just to be safe. "We need answers," Devin said. "We need to know what the *hell* is going on."

"Wait," CJ said, remembering what he'd heard from the basement when Jen had stopped by. He searched around for the box she had been talking about, and when he found it, he held up the tape inside. "I think the answers are in here."

Along the spine of the old videotape, the words *Camp Nightmare* were written in marker. Devin remembered Hannah calling the fort by that same name.

"It's a videotape from, like, a hundred years ago," Cece said.

"I know where we can play this," Devin said. "Come on!"

Just as they raced toward the steps of the nearest subway station, Alex came chasing after them. "What are you doing here?" Cece asked, remembering their awful conversation from the park earlier that afternoon.

"Frankie texted me," Alex said simply.

"I thought you didn't want anything to do with us," Cece reminded her.

"I want to know what's on my mom's tape," Alex said firmly.

Cece smiled at her. "The more the merrier."

Trey looked around at the group who were gathering together near the subway platform and said, "I feel like I missed something . . ."

Frankie nodded and looked at him lovingly. "I'll fill you in."

Just before the train arrived, Devin began to peel away from the group. "You guys go to Grandma's," he told the others. "I gotta get back to Hannah. I promised. I'm sorry, this is just something I have to do."

"Devin," Cece snapped. "Are you serious? After what happened to Dad?"

"Who's Hannah?" Frankie asked.

Devin lifted his chin. "A girl I met. I think she might know something about the fort that could help Dad. I'll meet you guys later." He took off before anyone could convince him otherwise.

Poor Anthony was still headless . . . and now he was alone, too. But sometimes, alone could be much better than *not* alone, and this was definitely true for Anthony at that particular moment. As he tried to roll his head back onto his body, Anthony suddenly heard the basement door open, and then footsteps echoed all around him as someone walked down the stairs.

Anthony watched as an unfamiliar woman in boots strode across the basement. He saw her put on a pair of latex gloves, the material snapping sharply against her wrists. "What are you doing down here?" he asked, just before the woman scooped his head off the floor and shoved it into a giant bag. "Oh," his head muttered as everything around him went black. "This is so not good."

CHAPTER TWENTY-FOUR

R amona Pamani had been living and working in her warehouse situated beside Fort Jerome for many, many years. She was a busy scientist, doing important work, but her work was private—very, very private. And she was determined to keep it that way.

Her only problem? The Brewer family.

Ramona pulled her Range Rover in front of the warehouse located just off the Fort Jerome property. As long as she could remember, she'd served as caretaker of the old fort, keeping an eye on things while also carrying out her own work . . . within her warehouse, and within the fort itself.

The inside of Ramona's warehouse home was an industrial, laboratory-type space. It was well-organized, but run-down, and not stuffed with the many comforts of a traditional home. Instead, it was full of chemistry supplies and plastic barrels labeled as HAZARDOUS, FLAMMABLE, and TOXIC. Filing cabinets and whiteboards rounded out the aesthetic. The space was just as Ramona wished it to be.

When she entered her makeshift lab, Ramona pulled on a thick, rubber hazmat suit before stepping into the warehouse's decontamination room. She settled into her space at the front of a large, metal table and studied her latest problem.

"Where am I?" Anthony's head asked her, still separated from his body. "What are you doing to me?"

Ramona began placing objects into a large vat beside the table. The contents of the vat immediately began to turn black and sludgy. Anthony didn't realize it was *his* body being dumped into the vat of liquid . . . until Ramona lifted his head and dropped it into the goo alongside the rest of his limbs and extremities.

Once his head and body were safely ensconced in the vat's liquid, Ramona began to make her report on an old-fashioned recording device. "Update on the 2024 outbreak," she began. "Subject B visited the site less than thirty-six hours ago. Unclear as to exact time of sporing. He was exposed, but the process appears to have been significantly slower than previous outbreak incidents." She paused, considering the next piece of her report. "When I found Subject B, the transformation was not complete. I have begun testing my containment hypothesis. I have commenced artificially speeding up the alien process."

Suddenly, a loud gurgle issued forth from inside the vat as Anthony's head bobbed back up and out of the black goo. Ramona reached over and, with her gloved hand, pushed it back down into the vat.

She still had work to do here.

CHAPTER TWENTY-FIVE

Cece, Alex, Frankie, Trey, and CJ were all huddled around the old TV at Cece and Devin's grandma's place. They were eager to watch the video labeled *Camp Nightmare*, but equally terrified about what was on the tape that had been buried and forgotten for the past thirty years. CJ was fiddling with the old video player, but he couldn't seem to figure out how to work it.

Grandma Naomi sat nearby, watching them with a vacant expression. "We're trying to watch something," Cece explained, but there was little point. Her grandma had little to no recognition of anything around her anymore; it was heartbreaking to see how much her dementia and memory loss had progressed.

"Who are you, again?" Grandma Naomi asked Cece.

Cece chewed her lip. "Cece. Your granddaughter." She took her grandma's hand in her own. Alex shot her a sympathetic look.

Suddenly, Trey stood up and shot out of the room. He looked like he was about to throw up. Frankie dashed out into the hall after him and asked, "Are you feeling okay? Should I call your dad?"

Trey righted himself and told her, "No, just got dizzy. I'm fine now. I guess it's the aftereffects of . . . whatever you would call what they did to my body." He shook his head, confused. "Maybe I'm freaked out about what we're going to see." He glanced at Frankie and begged, "Don't call my dad. The last thing I need is him feeling worse than he already does. He keeps asking me what happened, and I think it freaks him out more than me that I don't know."

Frankie squeezed his hand.

Just then, CJ called out from inside Grandma Naomi's room, "Got it!"

Frankie and Trey hurried back to their friends. Everyone was huddled on the couch, ready to watch. "Here we go," Cece said nervously. CJ pressed play, and the screen glowed as the Brewer home from 1994 appeared on-screen. At first, the footage showed a bunch of regular daily life scenes from Anthony and Matty's childhood. Cece thought it was surreal to see their dad as a teenager, their grandma as a young and dementia-free middle-aged mom, and their uncle . . . still alive.

Uncle Matty had borrowed the camera from his dad—Cece and Devin's grandpa—on the pretense that he would be using it for a school project.

After the scenes inside their grandparents' house, the teens watched as the video suddenly shifted to some kind of warehouse near the old fort. Anthony—their dad, also known back then as Stink—filmed through a crack in the door as Uncle Matty went into the warehouse and talked to a mystery woman. "I'm doing a class assignment on the history of Gravesend," he explained to her. "Really exciting subject. An opportunity to learn more about, um, the place where I live. To understand . . . my legacy. And what better place to start than Fort Jerome?"

The woman, who was clearly some kind of caretaker for the old, historical fort, didn't seem at all excited about Matty's project. "I think I have a brochure around here somewhere." She thrust it at Matty and said, "Here. That's all the history."

"Do you have a map?" Matty asked with a charming smile.

"Fort Jerome is private property," the woman snapped. "No one is allowed inside. That would be considered trespassing."

Matty shrugged, clearly trying to convince the woman to change her stance and give him more information. "It's just for my project—"

Suddenly, the woman noticed young Anthony and his camera through the crack in the warehouse door. "Who is that? What are you doing? You can't film here!" She ran toward Stink, knocking the camera out of his hands. "Turn it off! Get out of here!"

The teens who were gathered in Grandma Naomi's room all exchanged looks. Who was that woman, and why was she so protective of the old fort?

After the scene at the warehouse, the footage shifted to the school. Stink and his camera watched as Matty had his first conversation with a new girl who had just transferred to Gravesend from California. Her name was Hannah.

"I can't believe my dad filmed this," Cece said, shaking her head as the tape froze up. "It's so weird to see him as a kid. And Uncle Matty, he was just like . . . us."

"They're *all* our age," Frankie said. "It's different hearing the story and actually seeing them."

Grandma Naomi reached out to touch Cece's arm. "Where did Matty go?" she asked sadly. "Is it over?"

"No, Grandma," Cece assured her. "The tape's just stuck. He'll be back soon."

While the group was gathered in Grandma Naomi's room watching Stink, Matty, and Hannah, Devin was meeting up *with* Hannah— the very same girl the others were watching on their thirty-year-old videotape at the retirement home.

As Devin approached her, the comforting hum started up and he felt himself, once again, pulled into the girl's orbit. "Hey!" Hannah called out to him with an open smile. Devin sat down next to her, immediately getting lost in her gaze. Hannah waved her hand in front of his face and said, "Hello? Earth to Devin?"

Devin shook his head. "Yeah, sorry. I can't remember why I came here."

Hannah nodded. "You came here so I can take you to Camp Nightmare."

"Yeah," Devin said. "That's right."

"Let's go," Hannah said, then she pulled him up and off the bench.

Back at the retirement home, CJ was fiddling with the tape to try to get to the next batch of footage to play. "Why did your mom have this tape, anyway?" Cece asked Alex.

"I think she knew them," Alex said with a shrug. "I'm sorry. I don't know why she kept it."

Just as CJ got the tape running again, Frankie asked, "Is anyone else scared?"

Everyone answered at the same time: "Yes."

When the tape began playing again, the teens followed along through the school day as Matty convinced several of his friends—cheerful, up-for-anything Nicole and fearless Sameer—to join him on his against-the-rules exploration of the Fort Jerome tunnels. All of them watched, both horrified and fascinated, the three very alive teens who they knew would soon be the subject of a mysterious disappearance not long after their recorded conversation.

The final member of their group was Hannah, the new girl. "Maybe you can help me," Matty said, aiming his camera at her face. "I'm looking for a cameraman—or woman—to help me with a top-secret project. She could be new in town, that would be fine . . ." On-screen, Hannah smiled—she was obviously happy to be included in the group. "But she has to have a great smile. Oh, and she may or may not have a crush on this really cool swimmer-slash-basketball player."

Hannah rolled her eyes. "Okay, okay. Please stop embarrassing yourself. I might know someone who fits that description."

"Excellent," Matty said. As Cece watched, she realized her uncle had *game*. "Is she hot?"

"She's smart," Hannah said, grinning again. "Sooo . . . what exactly would I be filming? Is it, like, a doc?"

"We'll get to that," Matty said. "But first, I think we should talk about that crush you mentioned."

"Uh, the crush that *you* mentioned?" Hannah said, laughing as she grabbed the camera and turned the lens on Matty instead.

"What's going on here?" a voice off-screen asked. Alex bristled—she'd recognize her mom's voice anywhere. She watched as a younger, much more rebellious-looking version of Jen appeared on camera. "Matty, you want to introduce me to your little friend?"

"What do you want, Jen?" Matty asked, trying to edge away from the camera. It was obvious to everyone that there was some kind of drama between the two of them.

Jen smirked. "Wow, testy. Just because we're broken up doesn't mean you have to be so rude."

"Hannah and I are kind of in the middle of something," Matty told her.

Watching all these years later, Alex noticed that her mom looked uncomfortable for a moment, but then she regained her composure. "I thought you were going to call me last night."

Matty shrugged. "I got distracted."

From behind the camera, Hannah giggled. It was obvious *she* was the distraction. She continued to film as Jen stormed off, then she asked Matty, "That's Jen, the ex you told me about? She seems like a—"

"Unhappy person?" Matty finished for her.

"Yeah," Hannah said, laughing. "That's what I was going to say."

"Just stay clear of her, okay?" Matty warned. "She's unpredictable."

The videotape continued to play, but the scene cut and shifted to later that day, or possibly a different day. Now, Matty was the one behind the camera, and he strode across the park to where Hannah was sitting on a bench. "You made it!" Matty said from off-screen.

"Yep," Hannah said, putting down her book. "Your camera-person for the night, reporting for duty. Hand that thing over." She turned the camera to Matty, who was wearing a large backpack full of gear. "Are you sure Sameer and Nicole are cool with me coming tonight? I know they're Jen's friends, too."

Matty brushed it off, almost too quickly. "They were *my* friends first. And this is the perfect way for you to get to know them!" He glanced up and the camera panned to catch Sameer and Nicole walking toward them.

Nicole dropped her bag on the bench and said to Matty, "All right, spill. What's the big surprise? Where are we going tonight?"

Matty paused dramatically, then told his friends, "We're going to sleep over . . . at Camp Nightmare! We break in, set up camp, and we'll tape the whole thing."

"What?" Sameer asked, his fearless facade slipping.

"Guys," Matty told them, "there has been a standing senior dare for, like, decades for someone to spend the night out at the fort. Nobody has done it before. We can be the first. That's epic!"

Nicole gave him a high five. "I'm so in!"

The teens watching the tape cringed. They knew how this night would end, and it wasn't good.

"Nicole gets it," Matty whooped.

"That doesn't mean we should do it," Sameer pointed out.

"Why do they call it Camp Nightmare?" Hannah asked from behind the camera.

"Because there's some creatures who live in the fort that eat teenagers," Sameer said, all serious.

"Allegedly," Matty noted.

"Fine, whatever," Sameer said, trying to play it cool. "Let's do it."

Matty looked right into the camera and told Hannah, "I promise I'll protect you, okay?"

"Matty, wait!" The camera turned to catch Stink, racing toward them with Jen in tow.

"Stink, what are you doing here?" Matty asked, obviously annoyed at his little brother.

"You said you needed to borrow the camera for a school project," Stink whined. "But Mom told me you were going camping tonight. I know you're not camping. You're going to the fort."

Jen rolled her eyes. "I can't believe you're gonna do that stupid Camp Nightmare thing. Like, seriously?"

"Matty," Stink said. "It's dangerous. Don't go!" He turned and pleaded with Jen, "Tell him not to go. He's your boyfriend. You know you're getting back together."

Jen glanced at the camera and with a small smile, said, "Of course we are. We always do."

Matty leaned in toward the camera, just close enough that it picked up his voice when he said quietly, "That's not true, Hannah."

Then he told his brother, "Stink, I'm not listening to anything she tells me to do or not do. Just go home. Please. I'll be home in the morning."

The camera lingered on Jen's face, catching the hurt in her eyes when she said, "I'm leaving. I'm not wasting my breath on this loser. You want to go to Camp Nightmare, Matty? Be my guest."

Matty called after her as she stormed away, "Go make someone else miserable!"

"Matty," Stink said, pleading with his brother one last time. "It's not safe."

Jen spun back around and yelled, "I hope I never see you again. I hope you die out there." She looked straight into the camera and added, "You too, New Girl."

When the video flickered to black, the group watching from Grandma Naomi's couch all stared at the screen, speechless. Finally, Alex spoke up to say, "I guess—I guess my mom *did* know those teens."

CHAPTER
TWENTY-SIX

Devin was following his new friend Hannah along a dirt road. As they walked, growing ever closer to the old fort, Hannah grew more agitated—and more determined.

Devin, on the other hand, was getting increasingly disoriented. "Wait," he said, looking around at their surroundings. "How did we get here?"

"We're going to Camp Nightmare, remember?" Hannah said, beckoning for him to continue walking alongside her. "Come on."

"Why?" Devin asked, his eyes glazed over.

"To find your dad. Devin, hurry."

"He's there?" Devin asked, more confused than ever. "My dad?"

"Yeah, of course. Just like your other friend was. Everyone will end up there soon enough. Follow me."

Devin trailed after her. "Okay . . ."

Back in Grandma Naomi's room, the rest of the group was gathered around the TV watching Hannah's footage from 1994. She filmed

Matty, Sameer, and Nicole as the four of them walked purposefully toward Fort Jerome. It was night, and the video from the ancient camcorder was dark and disorienting.

"This way!" Matty called out to his friends.

"We're so lost," Nicole moaned.

"No," Matty said. "We just need to keep walking. There's going to be, like, a tunnel or something. I saw it in the brochure."

"Camp Nightmare has a brochure?" Hannah asked from behind the camera.

"Does it mention the ghosts of all the people murdered here?" Nicole asked.

"Wait, what?" Hannah blurted.

Matty shook his head. "Those are just urban legends."

The group continued to walk, but suddenly the camera jostled as Hannah spun around and yelped, "What was that?" Something had rustled in the bushes nearby—something large. "I thought I heard something," she said in a panicked whisper. "Someone following us."

Everyone looked around, searching for the source of the noise. In the dark, everything sounded bigger, scarier, more horrible. Suddenly, all of them screamed as a shape leaped out from the bushes. "It's a bunny!" Matty said with a laugh. "It's just a bunny."

They all began to laugh, but it was a nervous laugh. It was clear the gravity of their mission had hit all of them, and now the fear was setting in. "Sameer," Nicole said with a giggle. "You should have seen your face."

"All I know," Sameer said, shaking his head, "is that bunny better watch himself." As they all began to walk again, Hannah continued to film while they made their way along the abandoned dirt road. Sameer continued, "I'm just going to say, of all the weird ideas you've had, and that includes filling my parents' bathtub with Jell-O when we were six, this is the weirdest." He paused, then asked Matty, "Why are we doing this?"

Matty paused, then finally answered with a sigh. "Because if we do this, we'll never be forgotten. It's not like winning a few basketball games or swim meets. We'll be legends. And for the rest of our lives, no matter what we do or don't do, we'll have this."

The teens watching the video all held their breath after Matty said this on the recording. The truth of his words was horrifyingly tragic. He would never know just how legendary the group became on the night this video had been shot.

Hannah broke the solemn mood by pointing out, "If we survive, apparently."

Matty flashed her a smile, obviously grateful she found humor in the situation. "It can't be far," he told the others.

"We've already walked, like, twenty miles!" Sameer whined.

Suddenly, Cece began to fast-forward the tape. "What are you doing?" CJ demanded.

"This feels wrong to watch," she told him and the others.

"We don't have to," Trey reminded her.

Frankie nodded, then said, "Yeah, but we need to know."

As Cece continued to fast-forward through the lead-up to the events that took place inside the fort's tunnel system that night, she said to the others, "We know nothing happened to Matty and his friends on the way to the fort. We need to see the part where they get to the room where they disappeared. To save my dad, we need answers—now."

"Be careful," CJ said. The tape began to whine in the machine as Cece continued to jab at the fast-forward button. "This thing is like old people hair. You hit it too hard, it's going to snap."

Cece hit play just as the group on-screen was making their way into the tunnels. They watched the footage Hannah had captured of the tunnel system, the strange control room where something had happened to Devin, and then—suddenly—there was a loud noise as a shelf came crashing down. And then young Anthony appeared on camera. "Wait. Grandma, my dad was there that night?" Grandma didn't answer; she just stared at the TV blankly. So Cece moved closer to the TV for a better view.

"Oh god," Frankie moaned as the scene on-screen continued to play out. "This is tragic."

"They thought it was just a stupid dare," Trey murmured.

"They thought they'd be home the next day," Cece said, watching as her Uncle Matty guided her dad—little Stink—out of the tunnels and sent him on his way. While Matty was gone, the other three continued to explore.

"I hate this place, dude," Sameer said quietly.

"What's wrong with you?" Nicole said as Hannah panned the camera over to where the other two stood beside an old console. "This place is cool. Like, what is this thing?"

"A really old computer," Sameer deadpanned. "How cool." Nicole began to press buttons, and Sameer shrieked, "What are you doing?"

"Waking up the ghosts," Nicole said with a smile.

Suddenly, there was a flash of sparks and they all jumped back, the camera zooming in as Sameer began to panic. "Are you trying to kill us?" he snapped at Nicole.

"I didn't think it was on." Nicole shrugged.

Matty returned to the control room without his little brother just as the rest of the equipment in the room began to spark. Then something *popped* and everything shorted out in a chain-reaction electrical overload. There was a loud whirring sound, and Hannah turned the camera just in time to catch the movement of a circular hatch dropping away from the floor. There was an audible rush of air as the hatch slid open, then everyone began to cough. Hannah spun the camera around again and caught the moment when her three friends were sprayed with black spores that had shot out of the space below. "What is happening?" she whispered, backing away to keep herself away from whatever had just coated her friends.

Hannah dropped the camera then, but the recording still captured their conversation. "Matty," Nicole said, her voice shaking. "Your face."

"Oh god," Sameer moaned.

"Aughhh!" Matty wailed.

Hannah lifted the camera again, while whispering, "Guys?" She spun around, but her three friends were gone. They had disappeared; the only trace of them left behind was a pile of empty clothes on the floor where each of them had been standing. The room began to fill with a howling wind, and suddenly, Hannah was swept off her feet. The camera angle shook and twisted as Hannah was ripped up into the air and down into darkness. There was a loud clank as the camera hit some kind of metal below, then the tape went to black.

CHAPTER TWENTY-SEVEN

Just as Cece and the others began to wonder if this was it, if this was all they'd ever know about that night, the tape started back up again. The camera switched back on in pitch-blackness, then a light flickered on to illuminate the crumpled form of Hannah, just a few feet in front of the camera. She lifted her head and groaned. "Matty?" She crawled toward the camera and looked right into the lens. "What do I do?"

In the distance, there were noises—indistinguishable voices coming from somewhere in the distance. Hannah stood up and grabbed the camera, then called out into the black space in front of her, "Hello? Matty? Are you guys down there?"

The camera light caught some kind of figure emerging from the blackness ahead of her. She zoomed the camera in, trying to make out the details. Then, realizing it might *not* be him, she began to back away. "Matty?" she said again, her voice shaking. As she took another step back, Hannah didn't notice that she was stepping onto an open staircase. Just as she lost her balance and tumbled down the stairs, Hannah cried out, "Oh god!" and then the footage cut out again.

After one second of blackness, the video started back up. But now, Hannah had the lens focused on herself as the camera's light flickered on and off. "Please stay on," she pleaded. "Please stay on." The camera was the only light she had inside the dark, horrible space. She spun the camera around again, filming the room, clearly trying to figure out where she was. The distant noises were no longer there; the only sound the camera picked up was the ragged catch and release of Hannah's own breathing. "Sameer? Nicole? Matty? Where are you?" She spun the camera back around to capture her own frightened face. "They're gone," she said into the lens. "They're really gone. And there's something in here with me. I can feel it watching me. If anyone finds this, I'm Hannah Parker. And I'm sorry I ever came here—"

There was a creaking noise, and Hannah spun the camera around again. In the distance, there was a soft glow of light. Hannah walked slowly toward it, emerging into a room filled with pods. "What is this?" she asked, reaching out to touch one of them. The pods looked organic, almost as though they were part of some sort of enormous insect hive. But then, obviously sensing movement, Hannah spun the camera down the row to catch one of the pods vibrating. She zoomed in, and the video showed a transparent window at the top of the pod. She zoomed in closer, and there, inside the pod, was the frozen, black-eyed face of Matty. Panning to the next pod, and then the next, she found the people she'd been calling for in the darkness since falling down that hole. Her friends were trapped inside some kind of alien pods.

"No, no, no," Hannah choked out.

Crack! She spun the camera around, and the light caught the edge of another pod at the end of the row. The translucent window was cracked open, and it was obvious whoever had been trapped inside was no longer there. In the distance, the tape caught the sound of a strange, inhuman clicking. As a scream tore out of her, Hannah began to run.

The camera light bounced and shook as she raced through the underground bunker. Behind her, the sound of clicking grew ever louder. She couldn't shake whatever was chasing her. The light from the camera glinted off some kind of shelf or ladder, and it was obvious Hannah's only hope was to hide. Flicking off the light of the camcorder, she tucked herself behind the obstacle, trying to keep her breathing steady. In near complete darkness, the only thing the camera picked up on film was the bottom of Hannah's petrified face. There was a moment of complete silence, then the camera went fuzzy as something slammed down in the darkness.

Hannah's breathing intensified as she scrambled out of her hiding spot and picked up the camera again, this time pointing it away from her. She captured the image of an alien claw sticking out from under an object Hannah had thrown to protect herself. "What the hell is that?" she squeaked.

The camera cut out, then flicked on again to capture Hannah running up the stairs, then along the catwalk she'd first fallen onto. Crying, she slammed into the ladder and began to crawl back up, desperate for escape. The video footage swung as she dragged the camera up the ladder behind her. She got to the top and shoved the camera through the hatch first, so she could use both hands to hoist herself up into the underground bunker where this had all started. The camera rolled, then came to a stop a few feet away.

Cece and her friends watched as Hannah dragged herself out of the opening in the floor. She crouched, gasping for breath as she sobbed. Suddenly, the clicking noise started up behind her again. Hannah's crying intensified, and she whispered, "No—" Then, suddenly, she was jerked backward and dragged down into the hatch by a ragged alien claw.

But a second later, the film captured her pulling free of the alien. She popped back out of the hatch and her eyes went wide. She cried out to someone she'd noticed off-screen, calling, "Help me! Help me!" Then a human in a hazmat suit stepped into the camera's view. Hannah cried out again, "Help me! Please! There's something trying to kill me. It killed my friends. Please!"

Hannah was pulled back, dragged down again into the depths below the control room. The woman in the hazmat suit strode quickly across the underground bunker, her boots clicking on the floor. But she didn't reach through the hatch to help Hannah; instead, she went to the console and tapped at a few buttons. Seconds later, the hatch closed—sealing Hannah's fate.

The woman then turned and rushed toward the camera and the piles of empty clothes. But before she could reach down to gather them up, footsteps echoed from somewhere inside the tunnel system. The woman turned and disappeared into the shadows, obviously trying to stay hidden.

"Matty!" Stink's voice cried out for his brother, desperately searching the darkness for the teens who had been there less than an hour earlier. He spotted their clothes and bags, then the camera.

Moments later, Jen entered the frame. She looked around, confused. "I told you if I drove you here it had to be fast. I knew I shouldn't have done this—"

Stink grabbed her, his fingers white as he clutched onto her sleeves. "They're gone! I heard a scream! And now they're gone."

Jen stepped backward, nearly out of view of the camera's lens. "What are you talking about?" She noticed the empty clothes on the ground and shook her head. "This is a joke. Matty is messing with us."

"No, he's not! He was just here! I was just in here with them," Stink insisted. "I'm calling the police."

He raced out of the room, and Jen moved to follow. "Stink! No! They could get in trouble." She stopped, then spun around and strode across the room to grab the camcorder. The footage stopped.

"Oh. My. God," Cece breathed as the video ended.

"Matty!" Grandma Naomi screamed as she shuffled toward the TV. "I knew they didn't drown. He was the best swimmer!"

"I'm sorry, Grandma," Cece said, crying as a nurse came in to comfort her grandmother. "I'm so sorry!"

The nurse ushered them out of the room so she could try to calm Grandma Naomi down. Out in the hallway, the group of friends stood, unsure of what to do or say next. Alex put her arm around Cece.

"Okay, I'll just say it," CJ said finally. "Fort Jerome is full of . . . aliens?"

Trey swallowed. "I remember being in one of those pods."

"Are you serious?" Frankie asked him. Trey nodded in response.

"What does this mean for my dad?" Cece asked. "Do you think he's an alien now?"

"Well, Trey's not an alien," Alex pointed out. "So maybe your dad will be okay, too."

Cece glanced at her phone, realizing it had been a long time since she'd last heard from her brother. "We need to find Devin. He should have been here by now."

While Cece texted him to ask for his whereabouts, CJ said, "You know that woman in the warehouse? I think I've seen her before. I saw her at the hospital outside of Trey's room."

"Really?" Frankie asked.

Before CJ could say anything more about the woman in the video, Cece got a text from Devin. "What did he say?" CJ asked. "Where is he?"

Cece read the text aloud. "Camp Nightmare." She quickly tried to call her brother, but he didn't pick up.

"Who did he say he was going to meet?" CJ asked.

"Hannah," Frankie said.

Alex gawped at her. "Hannah? Like the girl on the tape?"

"I mean," Cece began. "Is it possible that it's *that* Hannah?"

CJ sighed. "Seriously? With all the scary things that have happened over the past few days? I would ascertain that Devin is *definitely* meeting the same girl we just saw disappear at Fort Jerome in 1994."

Cece began to panic. "We have to go! Now!"

CHAPTER TWENTY-EIGHT

Hannah and Devin were walking along the seawall near the Fort Jerome tunnels. Suddenly, Hannah stopped. Devin peeked over the edge of the wall, which dropped straight down into the ocean below. Devin felt foggy and a little off-balance, and suddenly, he remembered his sister was waiting for him. "I should—I should call Cece. I was supposed to meet her. I need to call her and tell her—"

Hannah looked sharply at Devin. She was staring at him with an unnatural sort of intensity when she snapped, "No. We have to find your dad, Devin. And find the others."

Devin blinked, confused. "The others?"

Hannah ignored his question and said, "This is the only way, Devin." She pointed down to the raging ocean beneath them.

Devin glanced down, noticing that the water seemed closer now. Almost as if it were beckoning to him. He began to lean, so very tempted to jump, when he heard his name screamed out from somewhere nearby.

"Devin!" Cece shrieked. "Stop!"

Cece, Alex, Trey, Frankie, and CJ rushed toward the ledge

where Devin was standing. They arrived just in time to see him teetering on the brink, close to falling off the wall and into the water below. Devin called out to them, "Hey! Hannah is going to help me find Dad! Real Dad. She's going to show me where he is."

Devin's sister and friends gaped at him. Frankie turned to the others and muttered, "Does he think there's someone with him?" Because in their eyes, Devin was standing alone, balancing dangerously along the edge of the deadly seawall.

"Invisible girls now," CJ said, his voice shaky. "Okay. Okay."

Cece tried to keep her voice calm as she called out, "Devin, I need you to get down off the wall, okay? Walk toward me."

Devin began to do as his sister advised, but then he heard Hannah's voice say to him, "No, you have to follow me."

"Devin!" Cece called again. "Please!"

Devin yelled back to her, "I'm with Hannah. It's okay."

Cece felt tears welling up. "Devin, there's no one there."

Devin looked away from Cece, then back to Hannah. He pointed at her. "Yes, there is! Hannah—"

"No, Devin," Cece said again. "Hannah disappeared in 1994. She was one of the three kids with Uncle Matty. It was all on the tape." She paused, speaking slowly and carefully, unsure and afraid of what her brother might do. "The girl you see, she's not real."

With the truth spoken, Hannah's spell over Devin suddenly broke. Devin turned to look at her, his expression hurt and confused. "You're not real?"

Hannah was furious. "No! I'm real. Of course I'm real!"

Devin considered this. "What year is it, Hannah?"

Hannah scoffed. "It's 1994, obviously."

Devin shook his head. "It's 2024." Hannah's face shifted suddenly as her memories of that final night came flooding back to her. "I'm so sorry, Hannah," Devin said softly.

Hannah gave him a sad smile. "I really do think you're cute." She stared out into the ocean. Then she turned to Devin and said, "Don't follow me." With that, she turned and stepped off the seawall. Devin tried to grab her hand to stop her, but there was nothing to grab. His hand dropped through hers like air.

As Hannah disappeared into the blackness below, Trey suddenly grabbed Devin and pulled him away from the edge. "I got you," he said.

"Thanks," he said, surprised that *Trey*, of all people, had come to his rescue. Devin peered over the wall, but there was no sign of Hannah. She'd never even been there to begin with.

Cece knew there was no time left. Spinning on her heel, she said, "We have to go talk to whatever that thing is in our basement."

As they walked out of Fort Jerome, Trey leaned into Devin and asked, "You all right?"

"Definitely not," Devin told him. "But. Yeah."

"I hear that," Trey said, nodding. "Well, if you're about to fall off a wall again, let me know. I'll be there."

Devin smiled at him. "Thanks."

CJ leaned into Frankie and said, "Of all the things I wouldn't have predicted, I think Devin and Trey becoming friends is the strangest."

Cece and Alex brought up the rear of the group. It was clear to Cece that Alex was still reeling from what they'd seen on the tape earlier that day. "You okay?" Cece asked her gently.

"My mom always makes me feel like a screwup," Alex told her. "And look what she did. She hid evidence. And she's a *cop*." She sighed, then said, "Whatever, I guess we both suck."

"You're not your mom," Cece reminded her.

"I make stupid choices. I say the wrong thing. I mess everything up."

Cece nudged her shoulder into Alex's. "I don't think you mess everything up."

Alex snuck a look at her and said, "You liked me back and I messed that up."

"Did you?" Cece asked. Then she reached for Alex's hand. They stopped walking and Cece leaned forward to kiss Alex, who kissed her back. "I have no idea why I'm doing that in this insane moment," Cece murmured into Alex's mouth. "But it just felt right."

Alex laughed. "It did."

Tucked inside the warehouse's decontamination room, Ramona returned to the vat in her hazmat suit. She leaned over the top where she'd dropped Anthony's head in, listening for the gurgle that would signify that the tank was empty. Everything had been sufficiently liquefied and drained. Just a thin layer of sludge remained in the bottom of the vat. Her alien spore process was nearly complete.

Ramona beamed over her work and said, "That was a day."

She could relax now that she knew the next stage was in progress.

Meanwhile, deep underground, in the Fort Jerome alien facility, black goo from Ramona's vat flowed into an empty pod at the end of a row of identical white pods that were lined up, side by side. As the pod filled, the goo reconstituted into the full, intact figure of Anthony.

His eyes darted open just in time to realize he was trapped inside an unfamiliar space. He pounded on the glass-like casing of the pod, yelling for help, but there was no one to hear him scream . . .

CHAPTER TWENTY-NINE

FORT JEROME, 1968

"*Okay, Camp Nightmooners, welcome to Fort Jerome.*" *Garrett, a counselor for a pack of five boys, ranging in age from ten to twelve years old, led his camp group toward the seawall that stretched along one edge of the fort's property. "This is the next stop on our Civil War badge tour. Fort Jerome utilized four tiers of cannons with sixty-eight guns just below where we're standing right now. Boom!"*

The campers all jumped a bit, screaming at the sudden outburst from Garrett. He laughed, then continued on. "The fort sat unused until 1890, when the government conducted torpedo experiments here." Garrett led them up a spiral staircase, urging his campers to walk out to the edge of the wall.

"Is it safe?" one of the kids asked nervously.

Garrett scoffed; kids were such wimps these days. "Yeah, it's safe. Just don't jump off." The campers all hesitated, clearly nervous to walk out on the narrow wall, perched dangerously high above the churning ocean below. "You guys are pathetic," he muttered, then walked across the wall to the edge to show them how it was done. "See? Nothing to worry about."

Suddenly, all the campers looked up into the sky as something massive descended from above—and hurtled straight toward them. "What?" Garrett asked, turning around. Splash! He was showered with a wave of water as some mysterious, massive object crashed into the sea below. He glanced down and was shocked by what he saw. "Far out—" he began, but his words were cut off as he was snatched by something and pulled right off the wall. The kids all screamed in terror.

Garrett was gone.

CHAPTER THIRTY

GRAVESEND, BROOKLYN, 2024

The next day, Anthony was still missing. The last time anyone had seen him was in the basement the previous afternoon, when his head was rolling around separate from his body. But when they'd returned to the Brewer house after rescuing Devin from Hannah at Fort Jerome, Anthony was nowhere to be found.

Frankie popped over to the Brewer house first thing in the morning, and stood awkwardly with Cece, unsure of what to say in a situation like this. "Hey . . ." she began. "How's it going?"

"Trey's on his way over," Cece told her. "Apparently, he knows something about the woman who took my dad. So, we're just waiting."

Frankie nodded and followed Cece into the house. Cece veered off to curl up on the couch with Alex, so Frankie continued through to the dining room, where Devin was sitting at the table looking through an old yearbook. "You okay?" she asked him. She glanced over his shoulder and saw that he was looking at a picture of Hannah, taken in 1994.

"Hannah was so real," he said quietly. "I was having full conversations with her."

"Devin, it was all in your head. She's not alive anymore."

"I feel like she is," Devin said, still staring at the yearbook. "And I don't know how to explain it, but I felt, like, this really weird connection to her."

Frankie was hurt hearing this, but she tried to joke it off. "So, what, are you going to date a ghost girl? Is that the plan now?"

Devin glared at her. "I'm not going to date a ghost girl. Stop making fun of me. I'm serious."

"You were under some kind of trance. Think about what we've been dealing with; this is just one more thing."

"It's not like that," Devin pushed. "I think Hannah needs our help. And if we could help her, maybe we could help my dad, too."

CJ arrived then, and they headed back out to the living room. Cece looked around at the gathered group and said, "We just watched a video with proof of mutants created by the military."

"They're not mutants," CJ said. "They're zombies. Trust me, your dad was definitely giving off big zombie energy."

"I don't care what's under that fort, zombies *or* mutants," Cece said. "I just care about finding my dad, who is still missing—"

"And . . . in pieces," Devin clarified.

"We found Trey," Frankie said hopefully.

Just then, Trey came inside the house with his laptop. "Check this out. I found something." Everyone gathered around him and his laptop at the dining room table. "I knew I'd seen that lady before. This is that *20/20* episode my dad was in."

He pushed play, and his screen showed an interview with Joe Junior from sometime right after the teens' disappearance in 1994. After Joe Junior's segment, the footage switched to an interview with someone named Dr. Ramona Pamani—the woman they had seen in the hazmat suit in Hannah's video. The reporter walked alongside the doctor in the clip and said, "Even though the mother of one of the boys who went missing, Naomi Brewer, doesn't believe her son drowned, the caretaker of Fort Jerome was there that night and saw the kids go skinny-dipping. Fast-moving currents will pull people out to sea and oftentimes their bodies are never recovered."

The teens watched, transfixed, knowing that Ramona had lied about what happened. She was the reason everyone thought the four teenagers had drowned—but the video they'd watched the previous night proved she knew much, much more about what had gone down in the fort's control room in 1994. Ramona now spoke on camera to add, "I've been warning people for years to steer clear. There is a reason this site has never been opened to the public. There are not only the obvious physical hazards, but chemical toxins still exist from its early days as a military site."

Trey hit pause, then said, "She knew where I was. Where your dad was. She could be watching us right now."

"We have to find her!" Cece said.

Alex Googled her, but nothing came up in the search. CJ scanned the results, and said, "There's just one mention of a Dr. Pamani, but it's Dr. *Avi* Pamani. He wrote a book: *Global Risk Management: The End of the World as We Know It.* Unfortunately, it's out of print and not online. Maybe they have an old copy at the used bookstore—or the library?"

"Well," Devin said to Frankie. "Fake medical doctor or not,

this woman was at the hospital. Do you think your mom could help us?"

"Maybe," Frankie said with a shrug. Her mom worked as a nurse at the hospital. "We should try."

"I'll go with you," Trey offered. Devin nodded.

"Okay, Alex, CJ, and I will go track down this book," Cece said with a nod. "Let's find Dr. Ramona Pamani."

Trey, Devin, and Frankie approached the nurses' workstation at the hospital, where Frankie's mom, Lucia, was on shift. Frankie chatted with her mom in Spanish. "Mom," she said.

"Frankie! What are you doing here?" Lucia looked up with a smile.

"We need your help with something. We're looking for the doctor who treated Trey."

Lucia glanced at Trey. "Is everything okay, Trey?"

"Yeah," Trey said. "I just, ah, have some recurring relapses with my symptoms. The symptoms are getting pretty . . . symptom-y. In my spleen."

The other two gave him a look as Lucia turned to her computer and said, "Okay, let me look your doctor up." She typed something, then made a face. "This is weird. Dr. Jane Clark, the doctor who saw you, is actually a pediatric cardiologist . . . and you weren't having heart problems. Just a second." She called someone, had a quick chat, then looked at the three waiting teens. "Dr. Clark had her badge stolen last week. I need to report this right away."

Frankie was thrilled her mom was playing right into their plan. She moved to phase two: "If they showed us the security footage, we could help identify her."

"Okay," Lucia said, nodding. "Come with me." She led them to the hospital security office, where the head security officer pulled up the files from Trey's ER visit on his computer. "Okay, here we go," the security officer said, playing the footage. "Tell me when you see the doctor you described."

They watched until, eventually, Ramona appeared on the screen. "That's definitely her," Trey said.

"CJ said he saw her in a hallway by the ICU," Frankie said.

"Okay, I know that hallway," the security officer said. "It exits to the front driveway. We have a camera there." He pressed a few buttons, then the monitor showed Ramona leaving the hospital and getting into a Range Rover.

"Can you zoom in and get the license plate?" Frankie asked.

As the security officer zoomed in, Trey took a quick picture on his phone. When the security officer and Lucia hustled off to report the incident to the police, Frankie turned to Trey. "Did you get it?"

Trey grinned. "Yeah, I got it. We can run the plates on the computer at the shop."

"That sounds legal . . ." Devin mused.

"You want to find her or not?" Trey asked.

"That sounds great," Devin told him. "Thanks."

CJ, Alex, and Cece had also gotten lucky at a used bookstore near the Brewer house. The three friends began to flip through a tattered copy of Dr. Avi Pamani's out-of-print book in the back of the dusty old shop. "This is all about how the world has to prepare for what it doesn't know and can't see," Cece said, quickly summarizing the contents for the other two.

"How do we even know this guy's related to that woman? What if they just have the same last name?" Alex asked.

Cece flipped to the back jacket. "Look, here he is with his daughter: Dr. Ramona Pamani."

Just then, Alex's phone vibrated with an incoming text from Devin: *We found her.* He sent an address and told them to meet there. Apparently, Ramona had just left—driving off somewhere in her Range Rover.

Not long afterward, the group was gathered together in front of Ramona's warehouse. The six of them walked down the alley and stopped in front of a steel rolling door that was locked by a bolt and chain. "How are we going to get in?" Devin asked.

"I got that covered," Trey said, pulling bolt cutters out of his backpack. As soon as he snipped through the chain, the front door rolled upward and they slipped inside the building. What they found was a large, loftlike space with no windows, shelving stacked with old-looking equipment, and a single bed in the corner. Stepping through a plastic curtain, the whole group stopped short when they saw what looked like some kind of evil lab surrounded by plastic sheeting. Trey whistled. "Well, this certainly gives off supervillain vibes."

CJ shuddered. "Or veterinarian office vibes?"

Devin pushed through the back side of the plastic curtain and stepped inside Ramona's decontamination room. He spotted her autopsy table and shivered. It was disturbing, to say the least. He scanned the creepy space, then spotted a large plastic bin nearby. He opened it and peered in, immediately seeing his dad's clothes lying in a layer of sludge at the bottom. He was about to reach in to grab them when CJ pulled him back. "What are you doing?" CJ snapped. "That's a biohazard bin!"

"My dad's clothes are in there," Devin said, his face pale. "He was here."

CJ peered into the bin and cringed. "Or part of him was . . ."

"But where is he now?" Trey asked, flipping open a case to find vials of a mysterious liquid.

"Hey, guys," Frankie called out. "Cece found something." She led them across the room to where Cece was standing, holding open an old, leather-bound book. Inside were pages and pages of meticulous, handwritten notes.

"It's some kind of journal," Cece noted. "It details all her experiments. She's been writing in it since . . ." She flipped to the front page and looked up. "Entry day zero, 1969."

Devin looked over her shoulder and read the first page. "What is the Orion Project?"

CHAPTER THIRTY-ONE

FORT JEROME, 1969

"*Going forward, you will only be referred to by your numerical assignment,*" *Dr. Avi Pamani said to the four scientists who were gathered around him outside the tunnels at Fort Jerome.*

Dr. Pamani's daughter, Ramona, handed each of the scientists a case, calling out their new names as she passed them out. "Number Three, Number Four, Number Five."

"What's your name?" Number Five asked her.

"Number Two."

Number Three gestured to Dr. Pamani. "So that makes you . . . ?"

"The one in charge," Avi said. "Please suit up."

All five of them opened their cases and pulled out new hazmat suits. As soon as they were adequately covered, the group set out together into the Fort Jerome tunnel system. After walking for a distance, they entered a gleaming, brand-new control room. "Remember," Avi told the group as a final reminder. "This is a one-year mission. Once we go down, we stay down."

Ramona added, "There is no contact with the outside world from below. *This facility does not exist to anyone beyond the people in this room.*" She pressed a button and operated a series of dials, and moments later, a hatch in the floor whooshed open.

"What on Earth is down there?" Number Four asked as they all peered into the hole in the floor.

Avi looked at Number Four seriously and said, "It's not . . . from Earth."

Once they'd all descended the stairs, Avi pulled out a special key and unlocked a panel. The hatch closed behind them, sealing the group inside. As the team made their way off the metal stairs onto the floor of the underground research lab, the scientists all stared up in disbelief. For there, hovering twenty feet off the floor, was an alien spaceship. "This is the clean room," Avi explained, ignoring the elephant in the room. "Hazmat suits stay on in here at all times. You can access the rest of the facility through the decontamination chambers." He pointed to two rooms behind the wall, with glass portals that looked out into the clean room.

"So we're dealing with a contagion?" Number Three asked.

Avi shook his head. "We don't know what we're dealing with yet. That's why you're here."

"But it's a threat?"

"We don't know that," Ramona answered.

"Something warranted all the biohazard protocols," Number Four pointed out. "What was it?"

Avi led them across the room to a plastic curtain. Pulling it back, he revealed a large pod—and inside the pod was a human man. "Garrett was first contact," Avi told the group.

"He's alive," Ramona told the others. "We've been able to check his vitals."

"Let's get to work," Avi said brusquely.

For the next six months, the group continued Dr. Pamani's research, trying to understand the ship and its mission. Using lab mice, they tested various levels of exposure, observing the results as the alien ship shed spores onto the creatures.

Each time this shedding process happened, the group of scientists watched as the living object that had been sprinkled with spores from the ship decomposed and turned into black goo . . . and then, moments later, the black goo would get pulled back up into the ship. After this, the ship would drop a dollop of black goo onto the floor. That dollop would rapidly form into a biomorphic pod that almost instantly reconstituted the mouse inside it.

Little by little, the group began to learn. And to build a possible antidote.

"Prepare the four twenty-nine compound D serum," Avi said one day, after the mouse podding process was completed.

Number Five lifted a vial of liquid off a metal tray. "Serum four twenty-nine compound D coming up." He prepared a syringe filled with the liquid, then passed it to Ramona.

Ramona stuck the needle into the pod. "Injecting now." As soon as she'd injected the serum, the pod melted away and released the mouse onto the floor. The mouse wriggled, then popped back to life. Ramona clapped her hands and cheered, "We did it!"

As time went on and the human remained inside his pod, Ramona grew more and more confused about what the goal of their project truly was. She finally went to her father one day and asked, "Why haven't you tried our serum on that man in the pod?"

"You know how long human trials take," Avi explained. "First we need to try it on the ship itself."

"Don't lie to me, Dad," Ramona snapped. "What is the real purpose of the Orion Project?"

"To assess and contain," Avi reminded her. "You know that."

"I thought I did," Ramona said. "But I pored over the data, and that serum is a weapon. You're trying to destroy that ship, aren't you?"

Avi sighed. "If it means saving humanity, then yes, I am. A foreign entity has entered our ecosystem and we have no defense against it."

Ramona was frustrated. "We don't know that it's a threat!" she insisted.

"Really?" Avi snapped back. "Tell that to the man in the pod over there!" He looked at her seriously. "This is potentially life or death for every single person on the planet."

Finally, the time came to test the serum on the ship. While the other four scientists watched on from the observation room, Avi pulled several tanks of Serum 429-D out of a large metal cabinet. He connected one of the tanks to a panel in the wall, then pressed a button to begin the process.

Cylindrical tubes shot out from the walls and punctured the alien ship just as Avi turned the valve on the tank to begin the flow of serum into the tubes. As the liquid flowed into the alien vessel, the ship shimmered, and then its shiny exterior began to dull. To Avi's eyes, it looked as though the ship were dying.

He closed the canister, satisfied that he'd done what he'd come down here to do: contain.

As Dr. Pamani walked out of the clean room, ready to rest after a successful day's experiment, he didn't see Garrett's eyes snap open inside the alien pod.

Later that night, Ramona was startled awake by her father's hand shaking her shoulder. "Get up. Now." Ramona opened her eyes and saw that Avi was wearing his hazmat suit.

"What's wrong?"

"No time to explain," he told her. "Just put on your suit."

She suited up quickly, then rushed after her father as he moved down the corridor. As they rounded a bend, Ramona spotted one of the other scientists up ahead. "Number Five?" she called out.

Number Five turned around slowly, and Ramona's mouth fell open inside the helmet of her suit. Number Five's eye was dangling out of its socket, and black goo was dripping from the cavity.

Avi shoved the scientist aside, fighting back viciously as Number Five tried to attack them both. With a final blow, Avi pummeled him in the head and scrambled away with his daughter to safety.

"Dad!" Ramona shrieked. "You killed him!"

"It wasn't him anymore," Avi explained. "C'mon." Then he rushed Ramona past him to the clean room. Lights were flashing alerts all around them. Overhead, the alien ship was spinning violently, shedding spores with each rotation. As they raced past the pod where Garrett had been trapped for the past year, Ramona noticed that the pod was now nothing more than a puddle of black goo.

Across the room, Ramona saw two hazmat suits crumpled on the floor. Helmets labeled THREE and FOUR were sitting beside them. Behind the suits, two new pods had formed—with Number Three and Number Four inside of them, their faces blank and lifeless.

Avi tugged his daughter toward the stairs. "It's too late for them!"

"What happened?" Ramona asked.

"The serum didn't shut down the ship," Avi told her. "It's fighting back."

The father-daughter duo raced across the catwalk, rushing toward the hatch that would return them to the aboveground world. When they reached the ladder, Avi opened the panel to the emergency hatch release, inserted his key, and turned. "Go," he told his daughter. "I'll be right behind you."

Ramona climbed up and out of the hatch. She turned around, reaching out a hand to help her father up. "Dad!" she cried out. "Give me your hand."

Her father didn't move. He just stood still at the bottom of the ladder. "My visor cracked when I fought off Number Five." He lifted his visor, revealing a hairline crack in the glass. "I'm sorry to leave you with this burden. It's up to you now. And only you." Then he pulled out the key and ripped the panic switch from the ceiling, breaking it so it wouldn't work from the inside anymore. As the hatch began to slide closed, Avi called up to his daughter, "Think of the greater good. Contain—"

Avi's mouth opened wide, and his eyes began to tear black as the hatch slid into its final closed position. "Dad!" Ramona screamed desperately.

She was the only survivor.

CHAPTER THIRTY-TWO

"Wow," CJ said as they read the final page of Ramona's journal. "So the whole urban legend about Camp Nightmare . . . it was actually aliens. Honestly didn't see that coming."

Devin opened the case of vials Trey had found. He pulled one out and studied it. "Four twenty-nine compound Z," he read from the side of the vial.

"That's different from what's in the journal," Cece noted.

Suddenly a voice screamed out, "Get away from that!" They all spun around, coming face-to-face with Ramona Pamani, live and in the flesh. But she stopped in her tracks when Devin grabbed the case of vials. "You don't know what that is," she said, pointing.

"We do, actually," Trey said.

"We know everything," Frankie added.

Ramona sighed. She thought of everything she'd been through these past fifty-five years. The guilt, the loneliness. After she'd lost her father that day, Ramona had gone home to their warehouse—alone—and there, in the safe, she'd found a letter her dad had left for her, or whoever found it if she hadn't survived the bunker, either. It said: "If you are reading this, the Orion Project under Fort Jerome has failed. Which means I set in motion lockdown protocols. Under no circumstances must the hatch to the lab facility be opened—the fate of humanity depends on it. It depends on you . . ."

Ramona told the teens about the letter, and then said, "I have spent the last fifty-five years following my father's wishes. But in that time, the Brewer family has made it very difficult for me."

"Is our dad in that room under the fort?" Cece asked.

Ramona nodded. "That's what happens once you're exposed. The ship draws you back to it."

Trey looked shocked. "Is that what happened to me?"

"Yes," Ramona said.

"How did he get out?" Frankie wondered aloud.

"With that." She pointed to the vial of 429-Z. "Over all these years, I've perfected my father's original formula."

"That's how you saved me?" Trey asked. "You really were my doctor."

"So this can save our dad?" Cece said eagerly, gesturing to the vial.

"I'm sorry, but it's too risky to go down there," Ramona said apologetically.

"My dad is a scientist," Cece began. "And he has always said science should be the riskiest profession or you aren't doing it right."

"You remind me of a young me," Ramona said fondly.

"And you would do anything to bring your dad back, wouldn't you?" Cece asked her. "Help us. Please."

Ramona considered this. Then she said, "Okay, I'll help you. But we have to move fast. Your father is running out of time."

Ramona led the group of teens to the control room, walking purposefully to the console. She pressed buttons and flipped switches, causing the control room to light up and come to life.

"Guys," Devin said as he and the others watched Ramona work. "Cece and I have to go down there. It's our dad—"

"We talked about this," Frankie reminded him.

Alex nodded. "We're all in this together now."

CJ and Trey nodded, too. CJ said, "I don't even have a joke to make about it."

Devin was about to say thank you when Ramona reached out and shoved a massive needle into his neck. "Everyone gets an injection of the serum," Ramona said as Devin whimpered in pain. "This only protects you from being podded." She injected CJ, then moved on to Trey.

"What about the thing we saw on the video?" Trey asked. "There was something crawling around down there."

Ramona said brusquely, "I took care of it."

Just as Ramona held up a syringe to give Frankie her shot of serum, Frankie said, "At this point we're going to need something more specific than that."

"I killed it years ago," Ramona said, then injected Alex.

"With the same stuff you're injecting in us?" Alex asked.

"I've used it on myself many times."

Cece grumbled, "Why is that not comforting?"

Ramona gave Cece her shot, then said, "There's some emergency gear in that bag—flashlights, blankets. If he comes out of this, he'll be naked."

Trying to lighten the mood, Devin muttered, "The trauma keeps coming." Then he bent down and grabbed the bag of supplies.

"There is one dose left for your father," Ramona told them. "When it awakens him, it will also awaken the ship."

"The ship can 'awaken'?" Alex asked.

Ramona closed the syringe-gun case and handed the single remaining dose over to Cece. Cece headed toward the hatch. "Okay, let's do this."

"Set your phone timers now," Ramona told them. "Remember, if you're still down there when the serum wears off, make sure you're not in the clean room. I'm turning on the backup generators. I'll keep the hatch open from up here."

"Thank you," Cece said earnestly.

Ramona nodded, watching as each of them descended into the hatch—just as she, her dad, and their team of scientists had done all those many years ago. As soon as they'd all gone down, Ramona turned the key and punched a button on the console. The hatch began to slide closed. "I'm sorry," Ramona said quietly as the hatch slid closed. Then she walked purposefully out of the control room, cold as ice. With a curt nod of her head, she said confidently, "Contained."

CHAPTER THIRTY-THREE

"I can't believe she played us," CJ said as the realization of Ramona's betrayal hit the group now trapped inside the underground facility beneath the hatch. "Okay . . . I *can* believe she played us."

"So, what?" Alex asked, watching as Trey fiddled with the broken emergency exit keypad. "We're screwed?"

CJ stepped off the ladder and onto the catwalk below. "Very screwed."

Devin bent down and picked up a backpack that was sitting in the middle of the catwalk. He unzipped it and read the label inside. "Hannah." He glanced at Alex. "You're seeing this, right?"

Alex leaned over the railing and pointed down. "Um, yeah— are you seeing *that*?" The alien ship was there, floating in midair just below them.

"So what do we do now?" Frankie asked.

Cece began to march forward. "Stick to the plan."

When they got to the clean room, Cece gasped. For she had finally spotted her dad, helpless and lifeless, inside his pod. "Oh my god. Dad." She rushed across the floor and reached out, but Devin stopped her before she could touch the goo encasing him within the pod.

CJ, Frankie, Alex, and Trey were standing a few feet away, looking at the four teens from 1994 who were also encased in their own pods, trapped forevermore inside the old, abandoned facility. "I feel like I know them all after watching that tape," CJ mused.

"They look exactly the same," Frankie said. "Not one wrinkle."

"I was in one of these, too," Trey said, stepping closer to Sameer's pod. "I remember."

Devin snapped Trey out of his memory, calling out, "Trey! We need the case." He checked his watch, where the timer was counting down. Five minutes had already passed since Ramona had given them their serum shots. "We should get started."

Cece flipped open the case and pulled out the single syringe that contained the last remaining dose of 429-Z.

Trey reminded them, "She said if this works it will awaken the ship, so be ready."

Devin opened the duffel bag, preparing for whatever might happen. "At this point, I'm pretty sure we're ready for anything."

Cece pressed the syringe gun into the side of her dad's pod, injecting the serum into the goo around her dad's lifeless body. After a moment, during which they all began to wonder if perhaps it wasn't going to work as Ramona had promised, the solid black goo began to liquefy . . . and then melted away.

Everyone stepped back as Anthony fell to the floor. His body was crumpled into a fetal position. He was naked and completely out of it. Devin rushed to his father's side, quickly wrapping him in a blanket.

"Is he . . . ?" Cece began.

"He's breathing," Devin confirmed.

CJ squinted. "What about his eyeball?"

"I mean, it's there," Devin assured him. "In his head, where it should be."

Just then, the ship began to hum loudly above them. "Guys," Frankie said. "I know what awakening means." The others followed her gaze up to the ship, where they all watched as something unfurled from the bottom of the vessel. It was like an alien umbilical cord, a living tendril shooting out of the mother ship.

"We gotta get out of this room," Cece said quickly. "Now."

"Help me get him up," Devin instructed her. They dragged their dad away, just as the cord swooped down and swung viciously at them.

"Move!" Frankie screamed as the giant whip of black goo and spores narrowly missed them. They rushed Anthony toward the side door, where Trey, CJ, and Alex were already waiting for them. Alex swung open the door to the corridor, racing through and slamming it closed just as the cord hit the other side of the door with a solid *thwack!*

Back in Gravesend, Jen had asked some of her law enforcement connections to do her a favor and track her daughter's ankle monitor. She needed to know where Alex was, since she was more worried than ever. "The system was working," Officer Morales told her. "And then all of a sudden her GPS went dark."

Jen stared at him. "Went dark? How does it go dark?"

"Maybe it's on the same wireless plan I have. I mean, my phone drops out all the time."

"I can't get ahold of any of Alex's friends. She missed curfew. Anthony's missing. Something serious is up. I know it." Jen paused. "Could she have removed the monitor?"

Morales shook his head. "If it was tampered with, the system would know."

"How could this happen?"

"Maybe she's just underground somewhere," Morales shrugged. "A subway station. There's probably a reasonable explanation—"

Jen jumped up and raced to her car. There was an explanation, all right, but she was pretty sure it wasn't reasonable . . .

Inside the facility, Devin explored the old sleeping quarters Ramona, her dad, and the other three scientists had slept in all those years ago. He opened the closet, spotting Number Five's pristine hazmat suit—the poor dude had died because he wasn't wearing that thing. "This seems useful . . ." Devin mused aloud.

Suddenly a hand touched his shoulder. "Hey."

Devin jumped, spinning around quickly. It was Frankie. He

took a deep breath and said, "We're trapped in a facility with aliens. No jump scares. Please."

"I know," Frankie said gently. "You're right."

"The others find anything?"

Frankie shook her head. "The corridor is just a big circle. Only way out is through the main room."

"With the giant angry spaceship?"

"That would be the one."

Devin laughed, despite the circumstances. "You're really calm, considering everything."

"I'm not, actually. I'm terrified." Frankie took a deep breath. "My mind is all over the place. Like, what if I never get to have pancakes again, or see the sun, or hug my . . . mom? Devin, what if we—"

Devin pulled her into a hug. "We're gonna get out of here. Just don't ask me how . . ."

Frankie laughed, then she and Devin both jumped as someone's voice called out, "Hey." It was Cece.

Devin and Frankie both cried out, "No jump scares!"

Cece gave them an exasperated look. "I was standing there for a while, clearing my throat. Dad's fully awake. C'mon."

They followed her through the winding corridors to the facility's rec room, where the others were gathered alongside the twins' dad. Anthony was studying the strange red tracksuit he was wearing, trying to figure out where he was and how he got into this situation. "Dev? Cece?" he asked groggily as his kids rushed into the room.

"What's going on? I feel a little weird." Then he paused, and his eyes flashed as a memory hit him. "Wait, am I in one piece?"

Cece smiled. "Good news: yes." Just as she said that, everyone's timers ended and six different cell phone alarms rang out in unison. The immunity serum had officially worn off and they were still trapped.

CJ cringed and added, "Bad news: everything else."

CHAPTER THIRTY-FOUR

Through the glass window of the observation room, Anthony studied his brother's still form inside the pod he'd been trapped in for more than thirty years. His kids had told him the whole story of what had happened that night back in 1994, and Anthony couldn't believe he finally had the answers he'd been craving for decades. "He was here the whole time," Anthony said sadly. "If I had just kept looking for him . . ."

"It's not your fault," Devin promised.

Anthony crumpled into a chair. It was heartbreaking to see his big brother, frozen in time, when he thought he'd died so many years ago. "He's so young," Anthony mused. "I mean, look at his hair. He always had great hair." Devin and Cece both gave him a confused look. "I know that's a weird thing to comment on, but I'm kind of in a few different states of shock right now."

Trey nodded and agreed, "It is great hair."

Anthony's head suddenly snapped up to look at the others. "We've gotta revive them."

"She only gave us one dose of that new serum," Devin told him. "Which we used on you."

CJ was studying the old computer on the desk like some kind of prehistoric artifact. "And then she locked us down here forever. No food, water, or cell phone reception."

"Well," Alex noted. "Then not *forever*. Just a few days max. I'm just being honest here."

"Dad," Cece said. "What are we going to do?"

Anthony nodded. "Look, guys, I know it feels like we're in a tough spot, but here's what we're going to do . . ." He trailed off, then shook his head. "I don't have it. I'm sorry. I thought I might find it as I finished that sentence."

"We need to get the hatch open," Cece blurted.

"I know how to open it from up there in the control room," Anthony said. "From down here, there's just no way. This is even worse than I realized only a minute ago." Then he paused and put a finger up. "Wait . . . Dev, that first night you were here—the hatch opened, right?"

"Yeah," Devin confirmed.

"How? What happened?" his dad asked.

Everyone swiveled to look at Trey, who said, "How was I supposed to know that transformer would blow up when I jammed a pair of bolt cutters into it!"

Alex shrugged. "I mean, it would have been a pretty good guess."

Inside the rec room, the group gathered around a sheaf of blueprints for the underground facility. Project Orion binders were open on the counter. "When Trey blew the transformer," Anthony explained, poring over the material, "it cut power to the facility.

And triggered the hatch to open. That's why Ramona keeps power flowing into this place. It's a giant safe with an electric lock. All we have to do is figure out how to cut the power from in here."

Trey leaned in to study the electrical plans on the table, running his fingers along the lines.

"What are you doing?" Devin asked.

"I took a class in electrical engineering," Trey said, grinning. "Did pretty well, too. Got a C-plus."

"Anyone else have any electrical engineering experience?" Anthony asked, cringing.

"Whatever, I can read electrical plans . . . for the most part," Trey bragged. He traced his finger along a circle that surrounded the hatch on the drawings. "Look at this. Those four pedestals in the control room. They all connect. The entire ceiling opens when you turn them on. I bet that's how they got the ship down here—"

Anthony cut him off. "Trey, we only care about the hatch. Focus."

"Yeah, yeah, yeah, I got it," Trey said, still looking over the plans. "I'm just saying—all the power runs down into that observation room. There's a fuse box in the wall. Right there."

They all leaned in to see where he was pointing. "Okay, good," Anthony said with a nod. "Trey kills the power. Hatch opens. Everyone runs like their life depends on it, because, well . . . you get it."

"Guys," CJ noted, "the serum wore off an hour ago. We enter that room and we'll all be in pods before we make it to the stairs." Everyone glared at him, even though what he'd pointed out was true. CJ shrugged. "I know I'm usually the funny one, but that just had to be stated."

Anthony's eyes drifted to the hazmat suit belonging to Number Five that Devin had found. "Tell me again how Ramona's father disabled the ship the last time? Which canister was it?"

A short while later, their plan was in place. Anthony was wearing the hazmat suit, and the others were ready to run as soon as they got the signal that it was safe. "Maybe I should go with you," Devin told his dad.

"There's only one suit," Anthony reminded him.

"What if you're wrong about this plan, Dad?" Cece asked.

"If I'm wrong, it doesn't matter," Anthony said. "What matters is that you guys get out. You saved me. Now it's my turn." Cece began to tear up. "Don't worry. I'll see you in no—"

"Thyme," Devin cut him off. His dad stared at him and Devin pointed out, "That was a plant joke."

Anthony grinned. "I'm proud of you." He grew serious as the reality of their situation sunk in again. "Remember, as soon as I connect the canister and disable the ship—"

"Trey blows the power," Cece said.

"And everyone makes a run for it," Devin added.

Anthony headed toward the clean room, while Devin and Cece returned to the observation room. "You got this, right?" Devin asked Trey, who was assembling his tools on the table. The fuse panel on the wall by the door was open, and Trey had already begun inspecting the wires and knobs inside.

"He's got this," Frankie assured everyone. "Right?"

Trey nodded. "Don't worry."

Cece watched as her dad became visible on the other side of the glass. "He's entering the room." They watched through the windows as Anthony stepped toward the canisters on the other side of the ship. The alien ship was still and motionless in the air above him. Alex put her arm on Cece's back and whispered, "He can do this." Cece flashed her a grateful smile.

Anthony rolled the canisters toward the plug in the wall, then connected it to the hose from the canisters, exactly how Avi Pamani had done it over fifty years before. "Trey," Devin called out. "He's at the canisters. Get ready."

Trey's fingers hovered over a nest of red wires. "I'm ready."

Anthony braced himself, then pushed the buttons on a wall panel. The cylindrical tubes shot out of the walls and punctured the alien ship. The ship shuddered from the impact, and the cord unfurled from the bottom of the ship again. Noticing the strange cord spiraling toward him, Anthony quickly moved to open the valve on the canister—but before he could, the cord whipped forward and broke the valve. It fell to the floor, broken and useless.

Diving out of the way of the lashing cord, Anthony reached for the broken valve and snatched it from the floor. Shoving it back onto the canister, he turned it with a quick twist and the serum began to flow into the ship. Just before it snapped at him again, the wriggling cord began to harden and turn white . . . along with the rest of the ship.

"He did it!" Devin whooped from inside the observation room. "Trey, go!"

Trey grabbed a heavy tool and smashed it into the fuse box. Sparks erupted, then the console and equipment panels began to short and blow. Trey whooped, "C-plus, baby!"

The whirring of the power grid inside the facility began to slow, then stop. The generators powered down, and the red emergency lights were the only things illuminating the space, the only sound the satisfying *hiss* of the hatch sliding open.

The six teenagers burst through the door onto the metal landing, quickly beginning to ascend the stairs to freedom. Trey led, with Frankie, Alex, and CJ right behind him. But Cece and Devin were a few steps behind, waiting for their dad to join them. "Dad, come on!" Cece yelled.

"The valve's broken," Anthony explained. "I have to hold it until you get out."

"We're not leaving you," Devin insisted.

"I'll be right behind you," Anthony promised. "CJ, get them out of here. Please."

CJ tugged Devin and Cece up the ladder just as Anthony turned his attention to the pods that contained his brother and his friends. The goo inside each pod was beginning to melt away.

Cece and Devin reached the top of the ladder and dragged themselves up and into the old control room at the end of the tunnel, the place where all this had started—and where it was now, finally, going to end. "Dad!" Devin called. "Dad, we're clear. C'mon!"

Trey moved toward the console on the other side of the room

and noticed it was beeping. "Guys," he said. "I think there's another backup generator kicking in and this hatch is going to close on its own."

"Where is he?" Devin asked, beginning to panic.

"I'm going back down there," Cece said, moving toward the hatch.

Alex stopped her. "You can't."

"It's going to close," Trey pointed out.

"Why isn't he coming?" Cece wailed.

Just then, Anthony appeared on the catwalk below them. He had removed his helmet when the ship was disabled and left it behind him in the bunker. Anthony looked up through the open hatch and said, "Help them up." He stepped aside and Matty, Sameer, Nicole, and Hannah walked forward—all covered in the remaining blankets from the emergency duffel bag. One by one, the long-lost teenagers began to ascend the metal stairs with help from Devin and Cece. Anthony scrambled up after them, dragging himself into the control room just as the hatch slid closed.

"Dad," Cece said, her head swiveling from her dad to the four teenagers who'd been trapped belowground since 1994. "You almost died."

"I couldn't leave them," Anthony said. "I had to save—"

Jen stepped out of the tunnel right then, into the packed control room. With a look of total shock, she finished Anthony's sentence. "Matty."

CHAPTER THIRTY-FIVE

"So, you're related to Matty?" Hannah asked Devin the next morning in Anthony's kitchen. Devin had just handed her a kombucha, explaining that his sister didn't drink it anymore.

"Yeah . . ." Devin said, trying to wrap his brain around the fact that Matty was his uncle, even though they were the exact same age.

"And you live here with him?"

"We're just here for the summer."

Hannah took a swig of kombucha, then made a face. "Oh my god, the taste. I see why your sister stopped drinking this."

Devin cringed. "She actually stopped drinking it for another reason."

Hannah put the bottle down and studied Devin for a second before saying, "We've met before, right?"

"Yeah," Devin said, smiling. "We have . . ."

Meanwhile, down in the basement, Matty was exploring the now-unfamiliar space and had just pulled out a box of his old things. "You found your stuff," Anthony said, walking toward him.

"Are you Stink?" Matty asked, just as he noticed the calendar screensaver on Anthony's laptop that was flashing the year 2024.

"You know I hate that nickname," Anthony said.

Matty looked at him sadly. "I'm starting to remember what happened."

Anthony hung his head. "I ran back in and you guys were gone. Jen was with me. We called the police. They said you drowned. We looked for you, we tried. We tried, Matty—"

"I know you did. It's okay, Stink." Matty assured him. "So, my kid brother is old now?"

Anthony laughed. "He is. But I try to exercise and eat well."

"It's not working," Matty said with a laugh. "So, Cece and Devin? Those are your kids."

"Your niece and nephew."

"I'm proud of you," Matty said, sounding just like the great older brother Anthony still remembered from his childhood.

Matty moved forward to hug him, and Anthony sobbed, "I missed you so much. I didn't want you to go there that night. I had a bad feeling—"

"I'm so, so sorry . . ." Matty began to cry, too. But unlike his brother, who was crying tears of joy and sadness, Matty was weeping black tears once again.

Jen was waiting on the porch when Anthony emerged from the basement. "They're all coming around, Jen," he told her. "Matty's asking for you."

"I can't, Anthony. It's too much. I mean—I went to his funeral. I never thought—I just can't—"

"He just wants to talk to you."

"Anthony. This isn't just me catching up with my high school ex. We have four presumed-dead kids in your house! I'm a cop. We have to tell someone."

"No. We can't tell anyone. Haven't you seen *E.T.*? They'll take Matty away. I just got him back."

"What do you plan on doing? It's not a sleepover. We barely even know what we're dealing with."

"Exactly," Anthony said. "There's an alien ship under Fort Jerome. And it does not come in peace. We need to stop that thing, and the only person who knows how is Dr. Ramona Pamani."

"The woman who tried to kill our kids?" Jen blurted out. "Who melted your disembodied head? Who prevented us from finding Matty, Sameer, Nicole, and Hannah for thirty years? That woman?"

"*That* woman," Anthony agreed. "Please, Jen. This isn't a tape we can bury. It's time we confront this thing head-on. Together."

Once Jen and Anthony had left to try to find Dr. Pamani, the ten teenagers hung around in Anthony's living room, watching

TV. Suddenly, Matty sat up and said, "So, does anyone want to get out of here and go for a walk or something?"

"Dad said to stay here and not contact anyone until he gets back. He was really insistent about it," Cece pointed out.

"I know why my little brother—now *older* brother—thinks that, but these guys need some air," Matty argued.

"Yeah, I get that," Devin said. "You were in those pods a long time."

"Devin," Cece warned. "Dad will be back soon. They who are supposed to be dead can't be out walking the streets together."

"Fine," Devin sighed. "We'll go with them and split up. I can go on a walk with Hannah—just throwing that out there. Or someone else can?"

"Nicole is dying for a coffee," Matty said. "She's addicted. Still."

Everyone looked at Frankie, who said, "I'm not supposed to go to the coffee shop after hours." Then she shrugged and said, "Okay, fine."

CJ stood up and said, "I can take Sameer to get some food at the restaurant."

"There we go," Devin said, grinning. "That's a low-key plan if I ever heard one." He looked to Cece for approval, but she didn't seem convinced.

"And I'll stick around here as collateral," Matty offered with a smile.

It was a plan. Maybe not a *good* plan, but *a* plan. It's not like there was a how-to manual for what you were supposed to do after rescuing your long-dead uncle and his friends from alien pods. This would have to do—for now.

CHAPTER THIRTY-SIX

A cross town, Anthony and Jen approached Ramona's warehouse quietly, relieved to see that the steel door was already open and Ramona's car was parked outside. Jen pulled out her gun and led the way as they entered.

As they crept across the warehouse toward Ramona's workspace, they could hear her voice call out gently, "One more dose should do it . . ." Through the milky plastic sheeting surrounding her decontamination area, they could see that Ramona was talking to a patient who was sitting atop her worktable. "Can you follow the light?"

Anthony and Jen stepped forward and pulled back the curtain. And there, sitting atop the autopsy table in front of Ramona, was Dr. Avi Pamani. Alive, unchanged since 1969, and in a full catatonic state. Alongside him was a case filled with 429-Z vials, a dialysis machine pumping black goo, and a syringe gun. "You have got to be kidding me . . ." Anthony breathed out.

Ramona reached down and grabbed a tranquilizer gun off her lab table. She pointed it at them, but Jen was already pointing her own weapon at Ramona. "Put it down!" Jen screamed. "Now."

Ramona lowered the tranquilizer gun, and Anthony stepped forward. He glanced between Ramona and her father. "You hypocrite!" He turned to Jen and explained, "This is her father." Then he spun back around to Ramona and growled, "What you put all of us through . . . You weren't 'containing' anything."

"I can't keep doing this by myself." Ramona sighed. "I needed my father back."

"At the cost of our kids' lives?" Jen asked.

"Ramona?" Avi's voice was faint, scratchy, and weak.

"Dad!" Ramona said happily. Her father was finally waking from his decades-long trance.

"How . . . long?" Avi asked her.

"Fifty-five years," Ramona said, her voice choked with emotion. "I've been working on the four twenty-nine serum the entire time. I've perfected it—I did the human trial. It worked. That's how I brought you back!"

"Oh no," Avi said, his voice filled with emotion. "What have you done?"

"I saved you—"

Avi began to convulse, his body spasming on the table. "You didn't," he gasped. "You can't. It's been too long. I was wrong, Ramona. We shouldn't have contained them—" He began to shake his head, then choked out, "This isn't me— This isn't me!"

Ramona sobbed, "I just wanted you back. I didn't mean for this to happen!"

Suddenly, Avi keeled over and opened his mouth. A black-and-green sac poured out of his mouth just before Avi collapsed to his knees. Seconds later, the sac grew until it was big enough that the whole thing consumed him, devouring and overtaking the body of Avi Pamani.

"No!" Jen screamed as the alien body squeezer continued to grow. She fired her gun, but the bullets just absorbed into its skin.

"That won't work on it," Ramona told her. She grabbed her tranquilizer gun and the dart of vials, but before she could do anything, the alien body squeezer shot spores out of its vertical mouth slit—straight at Ramona. Ramona opened her mouth wide, hearing nothing but humming as black tears began to pour down her face.

"We gotta go!" Anthony screamed, pulling Jen's arm. Just before they dashed out of the room, Jen grabbed the tranquilizer gun and darts.

They raced through the warehouse, the alien body squeezer close on their heels. It clacked and clicked as it ran, knocking over furniture. Just as it was about to pounce on them, Jen turned and fired a dart.

Splat!

The alien body squeezer began to turn white and harden, just as the ship had when Anthony had turned on the canisters of serum. Moments later, the creature crumbled into ash. Before they could celebrate, the reality of the situation at hand hit them. They turned to each other and, together, yelled: "The kids!"

CHAPTER THIRTY-SEVEN

C J and Sameer rode down Sixteenth Street on CJ's borrowed scooter, holding a bag full of food from Gwen's. As they rounded a corner, Sameer tugged desperately on CJ's shirt. CJ pulled over, letting Sameer off the back. "I told you," CJ warned. "You haven't eaten in thirty years. You have to go easy on the egg rolls."

"I'm sorry, man," Sameer said, keeling over. "This isn't me. This isn't—" He retched and barfed up an alien that immediately consumed him.

CJ freaked out, squeezing the throttle to get away. But the alien charged after him, quickly catching up. The alien swiped at CJ's back tire, and the scooter slid out from under him. It crawled forward, hovering over CJ, then the alien opened its vertical jaws and dumped a load of black spores onto his terrified face.

Devin and Hannah stood together on the street near where Hannah's apartment was the last time she'd been inside it, back in 1994.

"Where did it go?" she asked, studying the massive construction site that was in its place now. "My apartment building was right there."

"Yeah," Devin said apologetically as Hannah took a few steps forward. "They keep knocking down cool old places to build luxury condos with acai bowl places in them." Hannah's shoulders began to shake. Devin reached out a hand to comfort her. "I'm so sorry." Just then, she began to convulse. "Hannah? Are you okay—"

Hannah's voice was hard when she answered. "Of course. Soon enough, everyone will know us. Everyone will be us." She pitched forward and threw up a sac that overcame her human form in seconds. An alien rose out of the sac and clacked its mandibles at Devin.

Devin backed away, into the street, as the creature crawled toward him. Just as it was about to lunge, a car slammed into the alien and sent it flying through the air. With a sudden realization that the same thing was probably happening to all the *other* teens from 1994, Devin set off running. He had to help his friends.

As soon as he reached Frankie's café, Devin threw the door open and saw that Nicole had already turned into an alien. This body squeezer had spored Trey, and now it was closing in on Frankie. "Devin . . ." Frankie whispered, her voice shaking.

Devin raced forward and pulled Frankie away. He then slammed down the roll gate, locking the alien inside the coffee shop. "Cece's still at the house with Matty," he told Frankie. "Let's go."

At Anthony's house, Cece, Alex, and Matty had been looking through old photo albums. When Cece went upstairs to find more albums, Matty went to the kitchen to get something to drink. Alex suddenly heard a bottle crash on the floor. "Hey, are you good?"

"Yes," Matty called back from the kitchen. "And soon you will be, too."

Moments later, Cece came down the stairs. She stepped into the empty dining room and called out, "Hey, where did you guys—"

Something grabbed her from behind and yanked her backward. "Don't move," Alex hissed into her ear.

"What's going on?" Cece whispered back. "Where's Matty?"

"There," Alex whispered, then pointed. Inside the kitchen, "Matty" was now an alien body squeezer. The clickety-clack of his alien claws pranced around the kitchen as he searched for his human prey. The creature climbed out of the kitchen and onto the dining room table, spotting Alex and Cece hiding in a corner. "Go!" Alex screamed, pushing Cece out of the way as the alien sprayed her with a shower of spores.

"Alex!" Cece screamed, then took off. She knew she had no other choice if she wanted to try to help them. She ran outside and ran smack into her brother and Frankie.

"They're all aliens!" Devin shouted.

"I know!" Cece replied. She spotted CJ's overturned scooter and his clothes on the street, then looked up just in time to see an alien crawling down from the front bedroom as yet *another* alien crawled out the front door onto the porch.

All three of the teenagers turned to run, but they pulled up short as two more aliens closed in on them from the yard. The aliens opened their creepy, vertical mouths and released a shower of spores on the final survivors.

A few minutes later, Jen and Anthony pulled up in front of the Brewer house and found the overturned scooter. She went to it, just as Anthony discovered Cece's and Devin's clothes on the street, alongside Frankie's. "They were podded . . ." Jen said, her voice somber.

"Sameer, Hannah, Nicole, and Matty must have been implanted like Ramona's dad."

"Oh god," Jen choked out. "Alex. We're too late."

Anthony shook his head resolutely. "Not yet." He raced to Jen's car and urged her to get in. It was time to fight back.

CHAPTER THIRTY-EIGHT

While Devin, Cece, Alex, CJ, Frankie, Trey, and Ramona lay motionless inside their pods below the alien spaceship, Jen and Anthony moved fast. They pulled up outside Ramona's warehouse and Anthony raced in to grab a 429-Z canister, a syringe gun, and a case filled with serum darts.

"Why will it be different this time?" Jen asked him.

"Because that was never Matty or Hannah or any of them. They were in there too long, like Avi. Which is why it worked on Trey. It worked on me. And it will work on our kids."

He placed the canister down on Ramona's desk, right next to her journal. Anthony was poring over her notes, making sure he was doing everything to the letter. "She perfected the serum," Anthony told Jen. "We just need to run Avi's experiment again—this time, it will get rid of the ship for good and release the pods."

Jen opened the metal case containing the darts. There were only three left. "Three darts and four aliens," she noted. "Are you sure they're gonna be there?"

"Ramona told me—or rather she told my *head*—that everything goes back to the ship. They'll be there," he assured her.

Jen nodded. "Great." Then she slammed the case closed and she and Anthony headed toward the fort. It was eerily quiet and reminded them both of the night Matty had gone missing. But this time, they knew what was at risk—so the silence felt even more threatening.

Just as they approached the central archway ahead of the tunnels, an alien reared up to block their path to the entrance. It opened its mouth, but before it could release a spray of spores, Jen shot it with one of the darts. *Splat!*

Anthony spun around to look at her, in shock at the perfect hit. "I'm a cop," Jen said with a shrug. "It's what I do."

Just then, Anthony spotted something creeping up behind Jen. Shoving her aside, he sprayed the second alien in the face with the canister, melting it. "Not bad for a botanist, huh?" Anthony said.

Jen rolled her eyes. "C'mon."

Crossing quickly to the tunnel, Anthony undid the chain on the gate and it swung open. Just as they stepped through, a third alien leaped out from inside the tunnel, darting between the shadows. Anthony quickly lifted his canister, but before he could do anything, the alien swiped it out of his hands, sending the serum rolling away and Anthony to the ground. Jen shot the alien with a dart, melting it to goo. "That was our last dart," she reminded Anthony.

Anthony crawled over to grab the canister, saying, "Maybe the fourth one hit traffic?"

Just as he said this, the fourth and final alien appeared before them, stepping over the canister before Anthony could get to it. Jen and Anthony quickly moved into the tunnel and slammed the door behind themselves, locking it before the final alien could grab them. The alien lunged and clacked, slamming repeatedly into the gate. It gnawed and pried at the metal wiring, desperate to get through.

"This isn't going to hold for long," Anthony said, gesturing to the gate.

"What are we going to do?" Jen asked, staring hopelessly at the canister of serum that was now trapped on the other side of the gate. "The kids—"

Anthony considered the situation, watching the alien try to force its way inside. Finally, he had a thought. "We shouldn't contain them . . ." he mused.

"Trust me," Jen growled. "We should definitely contain them."

"No," Anthony said slowly. "Her father said he was wrong. He had it all wrong. Jen . . . that's it. We have to let it go."

"Let *what* go?"

"The ship," Anthony said. He raced through the tunnels to the control room, Jen hot on his heels. As soon as they were inside, he hustled over to the console and flipped switches. "The whole floor is designed to open," he told Jen. "We saw it in the plans."

"Are you crazy?" Jen screamed. "You're going to let the ship *out*?! What about the kids?"

"This is how we save them, Jen. It's about letting it go."

Jen considered this. Somewhere deep in her gut, she knew he

was right. She watched on hopefully as Anthony hit the same switch on all four consoles. Suddenly, a loud grinding noise rang out inside the control room and then, like a giant watch dial, the entire floor yawned open.

Moments later, the alien ship began to rise. It floated up, desperately seeking the freedom of the open sky after being trapped belowground for decades. As it rose, the pods around the ship's newest captors began to melt away. Its ascent grew more rapid, the ship spinning and spiraling upward. As it passed through the control room, Anthony was knocked to the ground unconscious. He didn't see the fourth alien melt away. As the spacecraft got closer, the alien turned to goo, then flowed upward into the belly of the ship, returning home before they made their final escape from the underground bunker. As soon as the ship was free, it blasted up and out of the fort and disappeared into the atmosphere.

Anthony remained unconscious, but in his fugue state, he had a vision. One final, fleeting meetup with Matty—who, in Anthony's dream state, he could see emerging from a bright light within the tunnel system. "I'm leaving, Stink," Matty said.

"No," Anthony pleaded. "You can't. I just found you."

"I'm sorry. I have to go. And you can't follow me this time."

"Please, Matty. Please. Don't leave." Anthony grabbed his brother's arm, desperate to hold on to him just a little while longer.

"You can't be there for me," Matty said sadly. "But you can be there for Cece and Devin. It's time to let me go, Anthony."

Anthony let his hand drop. He knew it was true. It was time. He could finally let his brother go, knowing the truth of what had happened, and knowing he'd finally found peace. He would never forget his brother, but it was time to say goodbye.

As Matty faded away, Jen shook Anthony awake. Her face lit up with a smile as she told him, "You did it, Anthony! They're okay!"

CHAPTER THIRTY-NINE

The craziest summer ever had finally come to an end. It was time for Anthony to drive Cece and Devin back to the city, and time for them to say goodbye to Gravesend—for now. "Cece! Devin! Let's go," he called out as he packed the last of their things into the car.

He skipped onto the front porch, where Cece was cuddling with Alex. "Your mom said not to be late," Anthony said. "But I want to take you to my favorite ice-cream place on the way back. Do you like yams?"

Cece tried to hide her look of disgust as she shared a smirk with Alex. "Uh, sure."

When Anthony went into the house to find Devin, Cece turned to Alex. "So, have you ever done the long-distance thing before?"

"I've never done any 'thing' before, so might as well give it a shot."

Cece smiled. "Okay, well, my first debate tournament is in a few weeks."

Alex frowned. "I thought you were done with that."

"No, I love it. I'm just done with doing it for any reason other than that."

Alex grinned at her. "Then, I'll be there. As long as I can be home by ten p.m."

Cece laughed. "Deal."

As Cece and Alex headed for the car, Devin and Frankie walked out the front door of the Brewer house. "I don't want you to go," Frankie said to Devin.

"Okay, then," Devin said with a shrug. "I won't."

"What?"

"I talked to my dad last night," Devin explained. "I don't want to leave him out here alone, and I'm not like Cece. I've always hated St. Agnes. It's full of, well, you know, Ceces. And I think I found my people out here."

Frankie beamed. "Gravesend High class of 2025!"

Devin nodded and smiled back at her. "I guess it's in my blood." Just then, Trey walked across the street. Devin stepped away from Frankie, still uncomfortable being with her when Trey was anywhere nearby.

Trey shook his head and gave them a look. "Guys, just be together officially, okay? You both want to. Just do it. I'm cool with it. Or *will* be cool with it."

Frankie glanced at Devin. "What do you say?"

Instead of hugging Frankie, Devin turned and hugged Trey. "You're my favorite Junior Junior."

Just as Cece hopped into Anthony's car to head out, CJ rolled up with his scooter. "I had to come send you off the proper way," he told Cece and Devin, handing over an order of egg rolls.

"I see you got your job back?" Cece asked.

"I even got a promotion," CJ bragged. "Apparently the delivery driver my mom hired is worse than me."

"Hard to believe," Anthony muttered.

Everyone laughed as CJ said, "Oh, look at Mr. Brewer going in for the kill again."

"I see what you did," Anthony said, pointing at him. "Solid punnery." Then he glanced at his watch and said, "We really gotta go. But all I can say is *thistle* be a summer you never forget."

"Dad!" Cece and Devin moaned together.

"What?" Anthony said with a smile. "You don't be-*leaf* me?" Everyone groaned, so Anthony threw one more down. "Oh my *gourd*. Everybody just *romaine* calm, okay?"

This got a laugh from everyone. Anthony beamed, soaking it in. As he pulled out of the driveway, everyone else headed out of the Brewer front yard. CJ gave Alex a ride on his scooter, Frankie walked home, and Trey headed straight across the street to his own house.

As soon as he got to his front porch, Trey let out a big burp. He frowned, then leaned over and spit up an egg sac onto the floor. His eyes went wide when he saw what had just come out of his body. With a slow shake of his head, Trey muttered, "That is not good . . ."

EPILOGUE

A few more weeks had passed, and things were finally starting to feel closer to normal again in the area around Fort Jerome. Devin was settling into his new life outside Manhattan pretty easily, but it felt strange not seeing Cece every day. As much as her intensity could make him crazy sometimes—especially in the stressful weeks leading up to a new school year—he missed having his twin around to roll his eyes with when their dad threw out corny plant jokes. Thankfully, Cece was coming out for a few nights to be Alex's date during Gravesend High's homecoming weekend.

He'd never admit it to her, but Devin was excited to see his sister. And more than that, he was psyched for the whole group to have an excuse to hang out again—or at least most of them.

The six of them were trauma-bonded for life, but things had felt different between him and the rest of the Gravesend crew since his sister had gone back to the city. And a lot of that was due to the fact that Trey had gone MIA.

Trey had been acting super weird when they left Fort Jerome that night. And none of them had been able to get ahold of him since. Frankie spoke to Joe Junior, and he said he and his son had gotten into an argument. His dad assumed Trey had left town to get some space, but the radio silence ever since that climactic night felt ominous. Devin had to wonder if Trey had disappeared because

Devin and Frankie were dating now. Trey had seemed supportive before he ghosted everyone, but Devin couldn't help but think something bigger was going on with his neighbor . . .

None of their other friends seemed super worried about Trey, though—and Devin guessed they *did* know him better than he did. CJ had his job back, and with the new menu he'd helped his mom put together, the restaurant was busier than ever, which meant CJ was hardly ever able to hang out. And between school and finishing her community service, Alex was acting all mopey, despite getting permission to hang out with Cece in the city at least five times already.

But more than anything, Devin was kinda . . . bored. Public school was way less intense than St. Agnes had been, and he had more time for nonschool stuff than he was used to. He half expected his dad would make him start doing nightly jigsaw puzzles or watch YouTube videos about botany together to kill the time—especially after everything that had happened with Matty. But instead, Anthony had been spending more and more of his free time back in the basement.

He had taken only a couple days off to rest and recover after all the spaceship craziness. But after those first few days of rest, it quickly became clear that even *aliens* couldn't keep Devin's dad away from his beloved lab for long. Maybe it was just the boredom, but Devin was surprised to discover that, recently, he'd been feeling a pull toward his dad's lab, too.

Maybe, just maybe, botany ran in his blood?

Or maybe, after everything they'd learned about Fort Jerome

and the decades-long project hidden within, Devin envied the way Ramona had gotten to work alongside her dad all those years. What would that be like? he wondered. Maybe his dad would be willing to teach him a few things, get him into plant stuff, and then they could team up—the Brewer duo!—to work on projects together, the way Ramona and her old man had worked on theirs?

As he waited for his sister to show up the Friday of homecoming weekend, Devin chilled on the front porch and considered the idea of working with his dad. It could be like an independent study project, he reasoned. Something to prove to his mom that just because he wasn't going to snooty St. Agnes anymore, he was still doing *something* important with his life.

While he mulled it over, Devin began to feel a familiar *hum* building inside his body. Even though the aliens were gone (hopefully for good), Devin still sometimes found himself caught in a nightmare set inside the fort. But that hum had been showing up during the waking hours more and more these last few days . . .

Devin shook his head, trying to get rid of the ominous feeling, but instead of going away, the hum began to intensify. He stepped off the porch, noting that the sound—a *pull*, almost—seemed to be coming from somewhere around the side of the house. Curious but cautious, Devin stepped carefully down the front steps and crept around the corner of the house. His ears peeled for the familiar noise, he homed in on the window with a view down into his dad's basement lab.

Devin took a deep breath and tried to shake off his paranoia before squatting down and peering through the brand-new window.

If he could get a look inside, maybe he could figure out what kept his dad so busy, day after day, now that all the weird stuff at Fort Jerome was done. Maybe his dad just had a new piece of scientific equipment that sounded oddly similar to the aliens' hum?

Devin's eyes scanned the room quickly, and he couldn't contain his audible gasp when he caught a glimpse of his dad, hard at work. For there, in the basement of the house that *he* was now living in, was a row of pods—not dissimilar to the pods they'd found inside the bunker. But instead of goo, these pods were filled with soil, like tiny little plant nests. Just like a collection of fresh seedlings, there were heat lamps hovering over each one. But it was what was tucked *inside* the soil that caused Devin to shiver.

Nestled in the soil within each pod was a small, gooey, egg-like sac. As Devin watched through the window, one of the eggs split open and a tiny green leg—one that looked much like the knobby vine on a pumpkin plant—emerged from within and took a first, timid step on solid ground.

But that wasn't the worst part. In the far, shadowy corner of the room, Devin could see another pod. This one was larger—human-sized—just like the ones in the bunker. Before Devin could convince himself it was another plant pod like the others, something glinted near the base. Devin squinted and spotted a shiny, silver chain beside the pod: Trey's.

Devin stumbled backward, wondering if he'd made the wrong decision when he'd decided to follow that hum and look through that window. Suddenly, he heard Cece's familiar voice call out from the front of the house, "Dev! Dad! You here?"

Devin clambered to his feet and sprinted to the front of the house as fast as his shaky legs could take him. Dirt skidded beneath his feet as he came to a stop in front of his startled sister. Devin heard his dad approaching from inside the house; they only had seconds before he joined them. Cece took in the dirt on Devin's knees and his panicked eyes. But before she could ask him what was going on, Devin hissed, "Whatever you do, do not go into the basement!"